The Unabridged Version

Mermaid's Treasure

Sapphire Songbird Series

A Novella

Anna Brentwood

DEDICATION

To my grandparents; grand, great, great great; Morris, Pauline, Harry, Rose, Eva and Samuel and all the brave, adventurous individuals who risked everything to leave past and country behind to forge new futures for themselves and all of us who have come after them.

ACKNOWLEDGMENTS

A huge thanks to the many who helped make this story happen; author, friend and inspiration, Maggie Jamieson whose tireless efforts for her fellow authors never wanes; my talented author colleagues at Windtree Press; Mercer Addison; the amazing Colton Long for his creative input; my husband Rod for his strength; my mother for being an inspiration, my readers, advisors and supporters who all had a hand in making this story the best it could be--thank you all so much; Dakotah Warren, John Warren, Stacy Hering Astor, Kellie Crowdis, Jakie Roylance, Lynn Goldie Sandler and my beta readers, May Selinger, Brian Greenberg and authors April Aasheim, Apryl Abbrams and Jessa Slade.

.

*"All that is gold does not glitter, not all those who wander
are lost; the old that is strong does not wither, deep roots are
not reached by the frost. From the ashes a fire shall be
woken, a light from the shadows shall spring;
renewed shall be the blade that was broken,
the crownless again shall be king."*

J.R. Tolkien

PROLOGUE

September 7, 1893
Reval Harbor, Tallinn, Baltic Sea

Rusalka-mermaid, named for the mystical sirens of lore, was, in her first incarnation, a glorious warship in Tsar Alexander's Imperial Russian Navy. Twenty-five years later, she was living out her retirement as a training vessel assigned to the gunnery squad.

Armed forward to aft with all manner of nineteenth century weaponry, from nine to fifteen inch smoothbore Rodmans to Obukhov rifled guns, the top and side heavy matron had willingly sacrificed speed and range for armor and armament, though in truth, the dear old lady had never fired a single shot in battle. That day, the skies were blue and clear. The sun was shining and the beach winds blew as light as a mothers touch. The skilled and hardy crew of the Rusalka, twelve seasoned officers and one hundred and sixty-five rugged crewmembers, were tending to last minute preparations and awaiting orders to depart. And only one man, Captain-Lieutenant Petya Yaroslav, the captain's right hand, would remember that something about that day was unusual; that his superior officer, the sensible and rigidly proper, Viktor Hristianovich Ienish, Captain second rank, was acting quite odd and completely out of character. First, the methodically punctual captain boarded the ship forty-seven minutes late with the excuse that he'd been to the hospital for a relentlessly painful headache. His usually tidy gray uniform was mussed; his neatly coiffed hair pecked, but most disconcerting was the look of dismay on his normally placid face. He hurried aboard, ignoring the multitude of expectant faces watching. Second, he barked at the captain-lieutenant to accompany him. Used to following orders, Petya Yaroslav complied, and though he was puzzled by Viktor's behavior and curious as to why they were headed below deck instead of to their immediate posts, he didn't ask. Nor could he not help notice the elaborate gilded and carved box the captain clutched under his right arm, as tightly as a barmaid her coin. Petya hardly gave credence to the incredulous tale the captain spouted once he locked the door of his cabin.

Exactly thirteen minutes later, captain and captain-lieutenant at their posts, the Rusalka sailed from the harbor at 08:30 for Helingfors, escorted by the gunboat Tucha.

And while a gale was forecast, there was nothing to indicate it. Their departure was smooth, two-foot waves and gentle breezes. Seventeen miles north of Tallin, the fleet ships were within a half-mile of one another. The waves continued to grow in size and force, but it wasn't anything the crew hadn't been through before. By noon, sixteen to twenty knot winds had the ship bobbing like a cork. Whale sized waves blocked everything but the agitated waters surrounding them.

Dropping Rusalka's speed considerably, the distance between the ships widened as the fierce Baltic storm strengthened, graduating to forty-knot winds.

The waves became rolling walls of water, twenty feet high and more, punishing as they battered the iron lady like a randy pugilist's fists.

Every hand was on deck, each seaman never more alive or equal than when challenging the seas, fighting to survive, to tell another tale.

Unlike her fleet escorts, the Rusalka did not appear in either Helsingfors or Tallinn the next morning. The commanding officer of the gunnery training squadron, Rear Admiral Burachecka, ordered a search by all available ships in the area.

Nine days into the search, the body of a seaman washed ashore. The lookout from the Rusalka was the only one of the men aboard the doomed ship to ever be found.

For one month and seven days onward, dozens of ships crossed the Gulf of Finland to search for the missing battleship and its' men, only to find broken remnants dazedly moving from the tug of the sea, lifeboats with empty mouths agape--—never to be filled.

Later, a court of inquiry dismissed the commander of one of the escort ships from service for leaving the Rusalka during the storm. Rear Admiral, Burachecka, was found negligent in ordering the ships to sea with bad weather on the horizon. It was concluded the Rusalka went down with her entire crew.

And, in 1902, on Kadriorg Beach in Tallinn, a granite monument of an angel, arms outstretched and pointed at twenty-three degrees, the course the Rusalka took towards Helsinfors, was erected. History records that there were no survivors, and to this day, flowers and wreaths are laid at the feet of the angel in honor of those lost men. However, history can be inaccurate; sometimes angels appear in the most unlikely of places and oft times the lost don't wish to be found.

CHAPTER ONE

December 24, 1893
Ellis Island, New York

Captain-Lieutenant Yaroslav arrived on America's shoreline on the eve of her Christmas Eve festivities. He was both weary and empty, a different officer than the one who'd boarded ship at Helsinki.

Despite the excitement of those around him, he was of no mind for celebrations. Well aware of the chill of the winter air and the fog from his breath, because he'd spent much of his childhood in the frigid tundra of Siberia he remained unaffected. At thirty-one years of age he was a serious, scholarly man older than his years, content being alone and unmarried. He thrived on living a simple military life of precision and order. He never would have envisioned becoming the lone survivor of a terrible shipwreck and failed mission, a ghost. Or being tasked by his captain, commander and comrade at the eleventh hour, with a mission that had not only puzzled him, but had succeeded in sparing his life. And, for whatever it was worth, changing it irrevocably and forever.

Only in retrospect does one think of the questions one didn't, but should have asked or remember words exchanged, and suddenly see significance.

He would always remember his country, his comrades and his captain. As boys, both Viktor's and his family were involved in Decembrist plots and had survived the uprisings. Exiled as rebels than later revered, they were forgiven and returned to their homeland, their lands restored.

And now, through some quirk of fate, his unwavering obedience had led him here, to this day, this moment. And, though he suffered survivor's guilt, feeling he should have gone down with his ship, he wasn't dead. Not in the conventional sense of the word anyway. After much anguish and planning, Petya Yaroslav, aristocratic son and descendent of a Varangian prince, of men with names like Vladimir the great and Yaroslav the wise, made the only choice he could; he left his mother country.

He could no longer remain a decorated officer in the Great Russian Navy, or the son of deceased but respected idealistic, aristocratic rebels who had believed in equality, willing to take a stance and defy a monarchy. Instead, he must become someone else; a civilian, a humble fisherman, bourgeoisie, a sometime ship builder with the common name of Pyotr Marchencko. The few family left to mourn his death would believe his soul resided in a watery grave deep below the Baltic Sea. He knew a man could plan forever, but life had other ideas. He accepted that one had to do what one must to adjust to life's changing tide. He would emigrate to a new land and take on a new identity.

The ship made its way towards America's New York harbor. Watching through the same green gold eyes of his doppelganger, both tied to the sea, he was a little awestruck at his first glimpse of the famous lady holding her torch. The mother of all exiles, the Statue of Liberty proclaimed with silent lips; "give me your tired, your poor, your huddled masses, yearning to breathe free."

Petya's eyes moistened, his chest filled with unexpected emotions. His strong heartbeat quickened as he stood steady on the deck. The magnitude of this new experience was humbling. Whether he wanted it or not, he was being given a chance for a new start.

The boat anchored mid bay as the crew readied to tender the passengers to Ellis Island. There were other ships and thousands of people. First and second class passengers like him could disembark and pass through Customs at the pier ahead of hundreds of others, spared from long lines and scrutiny of the less fortunate, those passengers traveling coach or steerage.

Despite being raised in privilege, Petya valued simplicity. He shared his parent's ideals that men should be judged by their worth, not their birthright; that no man should rule or own another. This new land, this America purported to hold those same high values yet, like any human endeavor, was fated to be rife with contradictions.

Touted as the land of the free and the brave, America was the country born from philosophies that posited all men were created equal. That all people were entitled to life, liberty and the pursuit of happiness. Yet he already saw obvious discrepancies between the dark and the white, the rich and the poor, and those who settled here longer to those like him just getting off the boat.

Satchel in hand, gold and valuables sewn securely into his shirt and pants, blade hidden in his boot, Petya had learned a valuable lesson in politics and philosophy and said a final, silent and emotional farewell to what was and what had been. From hereonin, Pyotr would stand in Petya's stead.

So, it was Pyotr who paused, took a deep breath, and clasped his bag tight in hand. Pyotr who walked forward, his gait slow but sure. Carrying hidden promises as the ground pushed back against his heels, Pyotr stepped up and off the plank and onto the solid soil of his newly adopted country-America.

America the beautiful. America the melting pot. America the land of opportunity. The air was contagious with promise. No matter the challenges, he vowed to forget all that came before. For here, with no past to bind him, he only had the future, and the possibilities were suddenly endless.

CHAPTER TWO

February, 1894
Lower East Side, New York

His first thought upon seeing her was that she was the most beautiful woman he'd ever laid eyes on. His second was that he would marry her.

He immediately felt uncomfortable with his foolish and unsettling fascination for the deli owner's pretty niece, yet he'd come to this deli for every meal since.

The owners were like he himself, Russian. The staff was friendly and the place smelled of home, of warmth and comfort, of grilled onions and beets and dill from the brine of the pickle barrels; from fish and meat, from cheeses and breads and all manner of baked goods.

"Pyotr, welcome, how nice to see you again." A woman as beautiful as any sea siren smiled at him, a pot of hot water for his tea in her hand. "Good to see you back."

He chuckled and said, "Considering I am here every day, I should be saying zat to yoo." He watched appreciatively as she set the pot down by his teacup.

She giggled. "I only help out here when I can, I have another job. Being here is just fun for me."

"Da, I do know you have other job. I hear you are artist with needle but unfortunately, I don't wear dress. Every day you are here, is how you say…better day for me. For aunt and uncle too. Nyet-no?"

Color rushed into her face and she tossed her golden hair even though, except for a few rebellious tendrils, most of it was bound into a tight coil of knots and twists. Her wide eyes were exotic, a warm amber that reminding him of Russian forests.

"I think you'd look silly in a dress, and I also think you sir, are a bit of a flatterer. No?"

The sound of her laughter lit something dark inside of him. "What is that word- flatterrrer?"

He'd been studying English since he'd arrived and

his understanding had improved, but many words still eluded him. Grateful the restaurant was not crowded; he paused gazing into her eyes. She stared back but finally broke the silence by asking him what he would like to order. Adding in an almost chiding voice, "And, I suppose first you will want your usual, borsht, with sour cream?"

He nodded transfixed, wondering if something was going wrong with his brain. And his manners. By rote, he ordered the roast and potatoes too. And, the challah bread he'd come to like. He didn't want to be predictable yet he was childishly encouraged she remembered the borsht and then rebuked himself. It was her job to be nice. He was a customer.

Keeping his head down, he couldn't resist stealing glances at the woman, a girl really, as she laughed with the clerks, bantered with her aunt and uncle and greeted patrons by name, escorting some to their tables, checking on others.

He had never been in love, yet he'd never felt as fascinated by a woman before. It was as if he were bespelled. To talk to her even as a good customer should be enough. To wish she might even consider him in a romantic light was foolish, stupid. Yet, he could not stop wishing it. The thought that she might be promised to another bothered him far more than it should.

Four weeks after his arrival, he began to understand much of the English. By eight weeks, he spoke well enough that he rather fortuitously landed a civilian position at the American Naval yard tending boats, cleaning up around the docks and maintaining engine supplies.

He learned the girl's aunt and uncle were Russian Jews and quite religious. She'd been orphaned and had come to live with them in America as an infant. Raised Russian Orthodox, he was more a man of science than supposition. He supposed the girl, Irena was of the Jewish faith too, their beautiful niece whom he could not stop thinking or dreaming about.

Even if there weren't the differences of religion, what would she want with him? He was a man of thirty-two with old world values, foreign and honed by years of rigid service--far too jaded for someone full of hope and innocence. But logic wasn't working for him anymore.

He'd settled in an old tenement apartment on the lower East side of New York, an older neighborhood populated by Eastern Europeans; Russians, Poles and Germans. His European counterparts were working class, or poor, or of the Jewish faith. Being of the nobility, he'd little experience with diverse peoples or people with a history of being persecuted for their religious beliefs or affiliations, their lack of means or perceived odd behaviors.

His first real comrade was his neighbor, a cheerful young German. Jacob lived in America for five years and made his living as a butcher, the trade of his father and grandfather before him even though in his country he'd been an educated man, an accountant. It quickly was made apparent that being a foreigner often meant not having the same opportunities as the "true" Americans--those who had been here longer and had assimilated better.

Pyotr understood men and their hierarchies. He knew such was the lot of an underdog, starting from the bottom. On the other hand, anyone here, no matter his or her birth could overcome such obstacles. Many did, succeeding beyond their wildest dreams. However, it suited him to be ordinary and considered the same as everyone else. He did not want to stand out.

Bringing him his check, before she turned to go, Irena said, "Pyotr, I know you are new to this country and are just getting settled in, but I never see you at synagogue. I understand you live in the neighborhood. Attending services is a great way to meet people."

She said she never missed Saturday morning services, and had the audacity to wink. "I hope to see you there someday soon."

"Da!" He blurted before he could think. Shocked at himself, he lowered his head and stammered, "Um…yes…maybe…maybe someday you will." He almost meant it.

Smiling awkwardly, his face felt as warm as a just out-of-the-oven biscuit. He hoped it wasn't red. He knew congregants didn't necessarily attend a church because of a deep religious calling but he didn't want to purposely be deceptive.

Still, the temptation to see Irena and accept her invitation was strong. He told himself, a belief was intangible. Was it anyone's business if he believed as they did or not, as long as he respected their right to believe as they chose?

He could well imagine his pagan and Christian ancestors spinning like tops in their graves over the very idea of one of their own converting or even considering attending a Hebrew religious service, but they were all gone and as far as anyone who'd known him before, he was gone too.

As he stood, he gathered his coat and his hat and braved one more look at the beautiful girl who had captured his heart. Who was he kidding? He wanted Irena for his wife. If sharing her faith or attending religious services would somehow make that possible, he'd do it even if his deceptive soul roasted in Hell for all eternity.

CHAPTER THREE

December 8th 1904
Manhattan, New York

Paulina Alexandra Marchencko, bristled with all the exuberance a petite nine-year-old body could contain as she arrived home from school. She raced up the stairs to the family apartment and opening the door, shouted, "Mama, I am home."

Usually her mother met her downstairs at the front of their building, but she wasn't there today to greet her. Odd. She called out again, but there was no answer.

Maybe she went to the store? Maybe she was at Bubby and Zayda's or Auntie Ruth's and had forgotten the time?

Paulina loved Fridays! Tonight was the sixth night of Hanukah too, which made it even more special. All around, a sense of holiday was in the air from the beautiful decorations in the stores, to the Christmas carols they learned at school. She wished she could celebrate Christmas too, it seemed such a wonderful holiday, but as Jews, they only celebrated Hanukah.

For seven days and eight nights every December, Paulina never got tired of her mother's potato latkes, of lighting the menorah, singing songs, spinning a dreidal, playing nut games and eating special candies like her favorite chocolate jelly rings. She loved getting money for her bank and a present each night for eight nights. But on Friday nights she most looked forward to hearing one of her papa's wonderful stories.

All day her friend's words blurred at times. Even the teachers called her out for not listening, but she couldn't help it; she was restless for the day to end so she could hurry home, help Mama serve supper, light the Sabbath and the Hanukah candles and wait for Papa to return from shul.

Last night, Mama had been feeling tired and had gone to sleep early, so Papa had tucked her into bed and kissed her good night. She'd begged him to tell her another one of his own stories, a new and longer story and one not from a book; they argued and she persisted, until finally, he stopped, grew quiet, and then told her in his deep, raspy voice tomorrow he would tell her his best story ever. That tonight, he had to take care of her mother. Tomorrow was tonight. She couldn't wait.

She loved hearing about his adventures by the sea as a boy, about how he took one look at her mother and knew that she was the woman he would marry. How they had fallen in love and married within three months of meeting one another, but the best stories were the ones he told her about ships and shipwrecks, mermaids, sirens, sea serpents, about kings and queens and treasures.

She reached high to hang her coat on the hook, taking a deep whiff of the delicious smells permeating the apartment. The aroma of her mother's baking, fresh challah, apple cake, cookies made with honey and almonds, reached through the air in patches that changed as she walked, tendrils of taste that on an inhale, tugged her very tummy.

The cholent, a stew prepared from fresh vegetables herbs and meats simmered in a big pot on the stove.

Paulina grabbed her school bag up off the floor where she'd dropped it. She ran down the hallway towards her room, but noticed a light on in her parent's bedroom. Something wasn't right.

"Mama?" She called out than peered inside the room. Mama's bedside lamp was on. She walked in to turn it off, and was startled to find her mother lying on the rug and staring up at her.

"Paulina, darling," she whispered in a voice so faint, Paulina could barely hear her. "I'm sorry I didn't meet you, bebleleh."

Heart racing, she felt scared seeing her mother curled onto her side with her arms holding her belly, her face as pale as the white of her blouse and her honey colored eyes dazed and dull. In a too quiet voice, mama explained she had a bad cramp and was waiting for it to pass. "As soon as it goes away, I will get up."

She closed her eyes even as she kept telling Paulina not to worry. "I've had spells like this before…it will go away…they pass soon enough."

Paulina sat down on the floor beside her mother, biting her lip and waiting for what felt like forever.

As if to assure her daughter she was fine, Irena occasionally reached out to pat her on the arm.

Grasping her hand tightly in hers, her mother took several deep, fortifying breaths. Opening her eyes, she looked as scared as Paulina felt and finally spoke. She said, "Paulina-darling-mine. Be a big girl…go next door…get Ruth…tell her…I need a doctor and to please send someone for Papa."

Paulina immediately jumped up and ran to do her mama's bidding; praying with all her heart her mother would be alright, not at all old or experienced enough to know that in life, even the most earnest and deserving of prayers aren't always heard.

CHAPTER FOUR

Six Years Later
New York Navy Yard

Pyotr was in the yard's commissary on a meal break. Thrifty, he always brought his own foods. This evening that meant leftovers of cold chicken, kasha, celery, carrots and a generous slice of day old almond cake lovingly prepared by his daughter.

The Navy Yard was a city within a city, acres full of places and people existing to serve the military, the seaport and its enterprises. It also appealed to the disenfranchised, the hard, drunk, lonely and disturbed. Randy young sailors coming off ships from ports around the globe were common here, as were the roughened men desperate to sate their appetites and spend their coin on the loose women and whores even easier found. Whether captain or mate, honest citizen or criminal, class didn't matter here on the docks. Survival depended on being good at what you did and being able to handle yourself in any weather condition, any situation. Pyotr had always been drawn to the sea and while working at the port could be dirty, dangerous and physically taxing, there was peace in anonymity, routine and hard and honest labor. His beautiful daughter gave him the added impetus to push on. For in truth, this past eight years he was a man living with only half a heart since losing his beloved Irena far too soon.

The current project required six teams of men pulling fourteen-hour rotations with short breaks and shorter jaunts home for sleep. They'd all been working overtime, pulled off normal duties to help rush repair a submarine that had been damaged in a collision that had torn off an upper rudder and damaged the hull. His two companions ate heartily while the discussions varied from personal to work to jests to quiet. The job was only supposed to take a few months but had turned out to be much more extensive and complex.

Feudy, the night supervisor was a bald, ruddy faced Irishman. He grunted, biting into a once plump but now shriveled and dried sausage. Chewing it open-mouthed, he exclaimed, "There's no way this tub is gonna be ready by the end of next month."

Considering the twisted metal and buckled supports they'd found and having to completely rebuild the rudder assembly plus replace a large chunk of the pressure hull over the engine room, no one disagreed.

James, a burly Scotchman and talented mechanic scratched his head. His hair, the color of autumn leaves was a bit too long. It shot out in wiry wisps around his youthful face. Nodding, his burr in force he trilled, "Aye. I don't remember a collision ever impacting the aft control surfaces like this one. You, Pyotr?"

Pyotr nodded, adding, "Worst I've ever seen."

He was an unofficial civilian advisor and had trained or worked with most of the men on the project, but where Petya had preferred the command of men, Pyotr loved working with his hands. He especially enjoyed welding, soldering and brazing and was excellent at it. His years on the job, his knowledge and his meticulous attention to detail had earned him flexibility with his duties and the regard of his peers and superiors.

He recognized most people who came into the

commissary, who belonged and who didn't. While it wasn't uncommon for someone to get lost and wander into the worker and civilian areas, for some unexplainable reason, his entire body came alert when out of the corner of his eye he noticed a stranger enter.

A fair judge of men, he guessed from the man's cap and coat that the short, stocky fella with bowed legs and a weathered face was a Russian sailor, though he wasn't in complete uniform and appeared too disheveled and dirty to be a proper one. Pyotr supposed he was lost or on leave looking for a tavern or trouble, but either or, it was midnight and he didn't belong here.

The man stopped about ten paces past the doorway and froze, staring in his general direction. The stranger's repeated glances bothered him more than it should. Pyotr didn't recognize him or meet his eye, but it was obvious he was searching for something or someone specific. Listening to his comrades with only half an ear, Pyotr finished his meal, vastly relieved when the disputable-looking intruder finally exited the premises.

James and Feudy flanked him as they left the commissary, but before any of them could react, the

Russian slid out of the shadows and without proper address or introduction, pointed directly at him. In a harsh accent, he said, "Yaroslav."

The word was more accusation than question. The man's light blue fish eyes never wavered from Pyotr's. He stabbed the air with an accusing finger, his fingernail black and dirty. Pointing, he said, "Yaroslav. You are Yaroslav!"

Paused and seeming unsure what to do, both Pyotr's companions looked at him. In a quiet but firm voice, Pyotr stepped forth. Facing the man he said in hybrid Russian, "Nyet, begging your pardon but my name is Marchencko, not Yaroslav. Pyotr Marchencko. Do I know you?"

Crossing his arms and narrowing his eyes, the man glared. He shook his head and said, "Nyet, you are Yaroslav!"

Louder. "From Yuriev. . . near Kiev!"

Pyotr glanced at Feudy and shrugged before turning back to stare at the man. Shaking his head as one would to a recalcitrant child, he repeated himself. "Nyet! Never lived there."

The man persisted, refusing to budge. "You haf sister and many brothers...Gregor, Stefan, Michel, Maker-"

"Nyet!" Pyotr interrupted. "You are mistaken. Am not who you think you know. I am Marchencko! Am only child. No brother. No sister."

"I know Yaroslav when I see one, Mashka," cursed the man in Russian, the latter term an insult when used familiarly by a stranger. With angry eyes flashing he spat. "You aristocrat bastards think you can own people-ruin them."

"Do I know you?" Pyotr asked again. He didn't want trouble but recognized it when it came calling.

"Nyet, but you will," said the man, stomping his foot, his bulldog face feral. "The name is Boris Kuznetsov."

Pyotr's quick mind weighed options. The man was short and angry. More often than not, small men had much to prove, but he was certain he didn't know the name or the man. Dressed in worn woolens, eighteen years of work-calloused hands and weather-toughened skin as witness, despite the man's vehemence and crazed babbling, Pyotr knew no one would believe he was not who he said he was. Not reacting was key and once again, he ignored the insult and this time in Russian, firmly told the man he was much mistaken.

Boris seemed to think it over for a long second

then stepped back making room for them to pass. As they did, he bowed and with a sweeping hand, apologized for the delay. Though either James or Feudy gave the man's veracity further credence, to Pyotr, it was obvious from the malicious gleam in the lout's eye, the insult, and the tone that he was not in the least convinced or contrite.

Running through various scenarios in his mind, Pyotr later determined the man was guessing at best. Though the man may have seen or known any one of his many relations, the ancient and prolific Yaroslav family had many branches on its tree. They were generally well placed or successful and tended to remain in Russia so Pyotr doubted some vague notion of resemblance could ever become a threat to him here. But, he didn't like it.

Fortunately, the man had misidentified him, not recognizing him personally, but he had hit on his marked resemblance to Gregor, who was not his brother but was in actuality, his third cousin. Gregor was a family black sheep, a powerful warlord in his region. He was immoral and a lawbreaker, and while this Boris might have a legitimate quarrel with his cousin Gregor, the matter had naught to do Pyotr.

Not trusting Boris Kuznetsov's intentions or his vehemence, being singled out for what was a probably a nefarious purpose put Pyotr on edge. It was only after several days went by without further incident that he relaxed, thinking that was the end of it.

But unfortunately, it wasn't.

The man started showing up in the same places Pyotr frequented, usually in the very early morning hours before dawn when few others were about. First, leaning casually and smoking outside of the commissary and then poised several hundred feet from the machine shop where he was working, eyeing him as a hungry wolf would a limp deer.

Each time he went out of his way to make sure Pyotr noticed him. He'd stare, nod his head and tip his cap then go. Outside of the supply yard when Pyotr was alone, reorganizing materials, Kutnetsov called out to him rather loudly-"Yaroslav"-- but Pyotr acted as if he hadn't heard him and just continued on with what he was doing. Another time, Pyotr almost ran into him standing outside the outdoor commode. This time, Kuznetsov made a show of throwing his cigarette to the ground, stamping on it as if he were squashing a bug and enjoying every crunch, madly turning his foot until what lay beneath was vanquished into oblivion.

Pyotr was convinced ignoring him was a better tact than giving him reason to think he was disturbed by his actions or intimidations. He recognized a bully when he saw one. He discovered Boris Kuznetsov was not well known around the docks. Talk was he'd been a seaman on a Russian cargo vessel that had left port a month ago, leaving him behind. Maybe he'd defected or maybe not. Pyotr learned he took odd jobs as he got them and roomed in a nearby flop.

Always cautious, Pyotr became more so, taking care to make sure he wasn't followed. He was no shrinking violet but he still blithely hoped the man would grow tired of his cat and mouse game. When one week turned into three, he knew sooner or later he'd have to do something about his takavarikko--attachment.

Sooner came on his first Saturday off in weeks. His best friend Jacob's bride, a mature and jovial widow named Rachel had accompanied Paulina to the city to shop after services. He and Jacob met up with them for brunch at Horn and Hardart's on Broadway. The automat was some distance from their neighborhood. Sipping the delicious freshly poured coffee, Pyotr's heart lurched when he spotted his pursuer boldly peering into the window.

When their eyes locked, concern for his daughter and his friends prompted him to immediate action. Excusing himself on the pretext of using the bathroom he detoured, heading directly outside to confront his stalker.

He stepped up to him and said, "Enough. What are you doing here? Don't you have better things to do with your time, Kuznetsov? I demand you stop following me."

"Or vhat?" The man chuckled as if amused. "Vhat vill you do? New country is free country, da? Here a man can go vhere he wants. Be who he vants to, but then, you know that better than anyone, Yaroslav, don't you?" He spit, the ball of phlegm landing close to the toe of Pyotr's shoe. Pyotr stepped back just in the nick of time.

Disgusted, Pyotr had to squash the desire to throttle the man, but he did not wish to cause a scene. That would not help him get rid of him. Forcing his voice to a calm he wasn't feeling, he spoke to Kuznetsov in Russian saying, "I'm not who you think. You will get no money from me if that is your game!"

The man appeared insulted and spewed his guttural and broken English like vomit. "Ah, I don't vant your dirty money, you foolish aristocrat. Your people ruin me! Gregor big man vith many eyes all over forbids me to ever set foot in mother country again. I am beaten within inch of life, tied and drugged, shanghaied on ship only to end up here in America, away from motherland, outcast forever."

"What did you do to…"

"Not your business," sputtered Boris.

"You are right," agreed Pyotr, his own accent deepening with his anger as he answered him back in English. "It is <u>not</u> my business but this man of whom you speak is <u>not</u> my brother!" He took a deep breath, exhaled. "Nor anyone I have <u>anything</u> to do with. Am in America long time now. Am sorry for your difficulties, comrade, but I am not responsible for them."

"You <u>are</u> Yaroslav," said the man. He spit again, this time hitting the curb. "You go far, pretending to be Jew. You are as much Jew as I. The young girl, she does have the look of you as well. Yaroslav eyes…cat eyes. No Jew has eyes like that…that color—that shape. Your daughter, I presume?"

Pyotr's fists balled. "Don't dare presume anything about me, you newdachnik-loser. Don't be ignorant. Many Jews have light eyes. Blue eyes. Green eyes. I am not cat eyes. Not whom you seek."

"Does your pretty daughter even know who you are? What you are? What she really is?"

At that, Pyotr turned white and lunged, his hands snaking up to grab at the collar of the man's coat. He yanked him close and ignoring his rank smell shook him out like one would a wet rag. His whisper in the man's ear was harsh even to his own ears. "Am warning you, Kuznetsov. If you go anywhere near my family, you will find more trouble than you ever dream of before this day. You go, leave me be. We have no argument. Don't bother me or mine ever again!"

With a quick push, he let go of the man.

His mouth agape and his thick brows raised, Kuznetsov stumbled than slowly backed away. As soon as he was well out of Pyotr's reach, he stopped to make a show of dusting himself off and laughed, a raucous, obnoxious bray completely inappropriate for the occasion. Pyotr's heart sank.

He sensed no good would come of this. Boris Kuznetsov was crazed, obsessed and his final words confirmed it.

"Nyet. This is not done, Yaroslav. Never! Not until someone of your blood pays. Not until I say it is done." With his threat hurled into the wind, the contumacious lout bowed, saluting Pyotr with his soiled cap before smacking it back hard on his greasy head then scurrying off like the addled dock rat he was.

CHAPTER FIVE

New York
Two Weeks Later

Pyotr gingerly removed his overcoat, scarf and hat and hung them on the hook by the door. He could hear the radiators throughout the house rattling and pinging. The warmth and welcome familiarity of his home embraced him. He sighed, content as a boat reaching safe harbor; he was where he belonged.

His neck, back and shoulders were stiff, his legs, and fingers and joints were achy and cold. He could feel every bit of his years in his bones and he was beyond tired, but even without Irena to greet him, just walking into the home they'd made together, knowing their daughter awaited him helped shake off the bitter sting of life's disappointments, of old age, misguided grudges and too much time working outdoors in the dank, darkness of winter's cold.

"Welcome home, Papa." Paulina called to him from the other room, her voice cheerful. "I'm so happy your shift ends early today so we could spend this evening together. It's been far too long since we've been able to sit down together for supper. It will be ready soon."

Having picked up the delicious scents of the food, his nose told him the same. She called out again, adding, "I'm in the kitchen."

He passed his desk where the mail was stacked and awaited sorting and the living room where she'd set up the ironing board by her mother's old sewing machine. He could see the condensation on the windows where the brisk cold of outside met the heat within. The laundry basket was brimming to near full with clean clothes to be tended, and ever rushing to keep up her studies, Paulina's schoolbooks and homework papers were spread out on the far end of the sofa.

That she tried to do so much herself pleased him, but he felt guilt that she had far too much to do. She should have had more time with her mama, time to be carefree and enjoy life.

Pyotr smiled when he peeked into the kitchen and

saw her, apron on, a patch of white flour on her face. He placed his lunchbox on the kitchen counter, wiped her cheek and with a peck to her forehead, moved back to drink in the cheerful sparkling eyes and large welcoming smile aimed up at him. "Lots of schoolwork, malyshka?"

She said yes and affectionately kissed him on the cheek. His heart warmed even more.

Paulina was not only a beautiful young woman on the outside; she was a good girl, a credit to her mother and a solace to him. She was loyal and giving to her friends and was always eager to help anyone in need. Her pleasant, even-toned nature was as much a part of her as the rebellious wisps of dark auburn hair that were even now escaping her constantly uncompromising bun.

Being orderly was not yet her strong suit when she was in the midst of one of her cooking efforts. The kitchen was a mess of pots and pans everywhere, dishes in the sink and cabinets and drawers open.

"How about I help clean up," he offered picking up a rag.

"Shoo," said Paulina taking the rag right out of his hand and gently pushing him out of the kitchen.

"No, Papa, I will do it!" He looked around, threw up his hands, his sense of order riled. "You have far too much work here, sladkaya—sweetheart and I am not yet too old to help. If you won't have me, both Ruth and Rachel offer all the time to help with household chores."

She wiped her hands on her apron and shook her head adamantly. "I know that, Papa, but we don't need to burden our friends with such mundane tasks when we can do them ourselves. I can do them. I will catch up. And, I enjoy taking care of our home. I like to sew and cook. I even like to iron. And as I am one of the best students in my class and on track to graduate, you need not worry."

He sighed. "Paulina, we both know Mama's fondest wish was for you to have education and graduate so you could have choices in life. She would not want you to spend spare time doing housework and chores. She'd want, as I do, for you to enjoy yourself while you still can, sladkaya."

She hugged him and smiled. "I do enjoy myself, Papa. I see Mina almost every day and Elliott at least two or three times a week. I help out at synagogue, tutor for English and don't forget, I adore taking care of you."

His voice was gruff but it lacked bite. "Before you know it, you will have husband and home of your own to take care of, in time, maybe children. Life grows harder in many ways as we get older. There is no reason you should be burdened with so many menial chores when I am more than willing to help or pay someone-"

"Papa, no!" She clicked her tongue and shushed him. "Housework and doing things for the people I love is what I like doing best. I don't have ambitions to be a nurse or a doctor like Mina, a suffragette or own a restaurant or a fancy store. I would not even want to work every day at Woolworths as a shop girl and you know how I love to browse and shop there. It happens to be good practice for me to do these things so I will be good at it when I have my own home. And, it is wasteful to give your hard-earned money away to someone else to do the things I am happiest to do, don't you see that?"

"Yes, I do, but--"

"But nothing, it is fine."

He didn't want to argue because he knew that even at the tender age of sixteen, his Paulie took her role as the lady of the house very seriously.

"Supper tonight," she happily informed him as

she handed him a glass of his favorite vodka, "is meatloaf, homemade applesauce, mashed potatoes and string beans with rye bread. You have time to wash up and change before dinner, Papa."

"That sounds wonderful, darling."

Her sweet smile got him every time and he knew, as she did, that he was wet sand in her hands.

He chugged his vodka, placed the glass on the counter and retreated to his bedroom as he'd been sweetly commanded to do. Paulina knew him well, his routine, what he liked to do to relax and he recognized his own ability to lead alive and well in his offspring.

By the time he returned, having washed and changed into more comfortable, clean clothes, supper was ready.

Irena had established suppertime as an important family ritual that both he and Paulina still cherished whenever his work schedule cooperated.

During supper they usually had long, lively discussions. When she was younger, an evening could never end without him having to tell her a story, but today she was sharing tidbits with him about her day, about school, her best friend Mina and her beau, Elliott. Mina and she were as close as sisters since age nine and Elliott and Paulina were inseparable since they met over six years ago when she was eleven and he a bar mitzvah at age thirteen.

Maybe it was thinking of them as children that made the conversation he'd had with Elliott just a week ago so very shocking at first.

He'd been leaving shul when the boy, even taller than he remembered him being, hurried over to him. Greeting him politely, Elliott then asked if he could have a private word with him.

Pyotr cordially agreed and they walked out together. He'd always liked Elliott. He was eighteen now, a friendly lad, intelligent with a pleasant personality and good looks, warm dark eyes and black wavy hair. He knew his father from shul, they were nice, hardworking people, second generation Americans.

To his parent's credit, the boy was personable and a good conversationalist, speaking first about the service, and the weather. It was when he paused; clearing his throat several times that Pyotr realized he was nervous and surmised somewhat amusedly that he must be arriving at the topic that had prompted the conversation in the first place.

"Mr. Marchencko, sir...I suspect you know I care

for Paulina a great deal. We…I have cared for her since I first set eyes on her in fifth grade and I believe she cares for me as well."

"That she does," said Pyotr with a smile. "I remember the day I first became aware of you as Paulina's friend and would be protector."

Both Mina and Paulina had convinced the boy to rescue Mina's cat, seemingly trapped in a neighbor's tree. Wanting to impress the girls and save the cat, Elliott hadn't hesitated to climb the large tree only to have the cat jump down after luring him to the highest branch possible. Balanced dangerously as it was, he'd barely made his way down when one of the larger branches he'd used for leverage snapped, leaving him stuck and dangling precariously. To his utter mortification, the whole neighborhood had come out to watch as the fire department arrived and had to help him down.

"The tree story," said Elliott, wincing even as he smiled. The story had been retold countless times but Elliott had a good sense of humor and laughed along with Pyotr. "Thankfully, I haven't had to climb more trees or rescue any cats since. I like to think I've learned to be more prudent and think about what I am doing before I act. Not that I'd hesitate to help someone or come to Mina or Paulina's rescue if they needed me to."

"Da, I am sure you would do the right thing," agreed Pyotr chuckling as he asked him how he liked working in his father's store. "Your papa is tickled to have you there with him, where he worked with his father before him. He tells everyone how talented you are. He jokes he can soon retire."

Elliott looked pleased and admitted he was enjoying the jewelry business too. "I wasn't sure the family business was for me. I thought about doing something else after graduation, maybe college or law school, but now it feels right. It feels like it is where I belong. My father has taught me so much and now that he's made me a full partner, I am earning a very good living and I have the opportunity to try out some of my own ideas. I am very committed to doing my part to keep the business growing and successful."

"That is good to hear." He knew Elliott was loyal, serious and responsible and had a good head on his shoulders.

Pyotr wondered what Elliott was trying to say considering he had cleared his throat for what had to be the fourth time. He finally spoke, hesitantly at first and said, "Sir. . .that in part was why I wanted to have a private word with you. I've been thinking about, uh, the future. I am saving my money. I want you to know…I want…plan to…hope to ask Paulina to marry me and. . . I'd like your blessing."

Pyotr stopped dead.

Elliott could have hit him over the head with a hammer and he would not have been more surprised. "My blessing?"

Elliott's eyes were as wide and as dark as two mud puddles. Smiling and looking earnest, he nodded. "Yes, sir. . .I am asking you for Paulina's hand in marriage. I love her. I will always love her. I want her for my wife. I will work hard and provide well. I will be a good husband to her."

Pyotr knew as certain as the stars came into the sky each night that Paulina and Elliott were fated, but he was in no hurry to think about losing his daughter. Certainly, not yet.

However, cognizant of the seriousness of Elliot's feelings and the nerve it required to approach a young woman's father, Pyotr was kind, but his exasperation showed through. "Paulina is not yet seventeen! She has not even graduated high school. Unless there is something you both are not telling me, don't you think you are rushing things, young man?"

Probably seeing Pyotr's flushed face and hearing the emotion in his voice, Elliott immediately apologized. Stammering, he tried to explain himself better. "Maybe I am getting ahead of myself. I didn't mean to imply I'd be proposing right now." He explained that he expected to wait, but he wanted to let Pyotr know his intentions. He hoped to surprise Paulina by proposing to her after graduation, but he wanted Pyotr's blessing first.

"She will be closer to eighteen and I expect we'd be engaged for at least a year so she could plan the wedd-"

"Eighteen. Much better plan," interrupted Pyotr taking a deep breath of relief as his heart returned to a normal rhythm. Understanding that there was still time to get used to the idea, he felt calmer and said, "You have surprised me, Elliott. You see, before having child, you don't imagine life having one. When you have child, each day is so full, you don't have time to think. They become part of everything you do and sometimes the very reason why. Before you know it, they are grown. It is never easy to accept they will leave. You understand that is the way of it. It is adjustment. It was important to Paulina's mama she have diploma. You may ask her after that and if she agrees, of course, you will have my blessing…son," he said, adding the last word tentatively.

Relieved and happy, Elliott agreed.

Pyotr nodded and, smiling slapped Elliott affectionately on the back. A relieved Elliott thanked him profusely, They shook hands and continued on their way.

That evening, the supper dishes washed, dried and put away, Pyotr sat in his favorite chair, smoking his pipe, sipping his vodka and reading the newspaper.

Paulina was standing and ironing clothes a few feet from him. Abruptly, she interrupted their companionable silence to say, "Papa, I almost forgot to mention it. Today, I had a somewhat unusual encounter with someone you might know from the old country—from Russia."

Frowning, Pyotr put down his paper.

"I was at the delicatessen bakery when I saw this rather shabbily dressed old man staring at me. He wasn't anyone I recognized so I ignored him. But, when I was fishing a sour pickle out of the barrel and could not find a single bag to put it in, he appeared out of nowhere and handed me one. I thanked him. He stared so directly-rudely almost, but I thanked him again and hurried along. I didn't think anything of it again until I went to check out. There were about five people in line before me and the old man was there. He had his own basket with some items in it. He ended up standing right behind me. We nodded at one another and I had the oddest feeling he wanted to say something to me and then he did."

Pyotr had a sinking feeling. "What did he say?"

"Prasteete…excuse me for staring and then complimented me on my eyes. He seemed very taken with my eyes." Paulina shrugged, looking mildly amused.

"What did he look like?"

"He was short, squat, a little rough-looking. He spoke with a very thick, Russian accent. He wasn't very clean and he wore a cap. I thought it odd he didn't take it off inside the store. Oh, and he didn't speak English well at all, but he could tell I was your daughter. In fact, he called me daughter of Pyotr. . ." Her face scrunched in puzzlement as she added, "And I didn't even tell him your name."

Paulina was young, loving and far too trusting.

Pyotr didn't want to alarm her though his own saliva thickened in his throat and his heart sped up. Quietly, he said, "Paulina, you should not be talking to strangers, especially…how do you know this person didn't speak English? What did he say his name was?"

"Papa." She rolled her eyes and sighed with impatience. "I am not a child anymore and I walk about all the time. I was perfectly safe. It was daylight and I was in the middle of the deli in our neighborhood in full view of about 30 other people. I knew the man didn't speak much English because when I answered him back in Russian, he was very pleased. We conversed in Russian. I don't think he has been here very long. He looked alone and very out of place. If anything, I felt a little sorry for him. Aside from knowing your name without my telling him…he said the oddest thing…something about the people you think you know the most are the ones you know the least…I couldn't make any sense of it. Maybe it showed on my face, because he never did tell me his name, although he did say to tell you that he hasn't forgotten anything. Oh, and that he looks forward to seeing you again very, very soon, maybe even tomorrow."

CHAPTER SIX

Pyotr debated with himself whether to tell Paulina to avoid the stranger or not say anything at all. Instead, he told her he thought he knew of whom she was speaking. They both had to get up early so their evening ended shortly thereafter.

He bussed her cheek and wished her a pleasant night's sleep. She knew he would leave for work before dawn kissed the sky, long before she would be up for school, but he'd be leaving much earlier than that.

Fists clenched, chest tight, Pyotr paced in his room like a circus bear.

The bedroom remained as it had been when his wife was alive. The heavy velvet curtains of gold she'd made covering the windows, the matching bedspread, the wooden nightstand and reading lamp on his side, the bureau and the black and hammered gold trunk at the foot of the bed filled with who knew what. He'd opted not to say anything at all to Paulina. He didn't want to burden her with worry or fear though he'd felt the roar of paternal protection rise in his chest the moment she started telling him about her encounter with Boris Kuznetsov.

He felt like hitting something—someone—Boris Kuznetsov. The man was a boil on the ass of mankind, dog-shit, a cockroach and very apparently a threat. Slamming his fist down on the bed as to not alarm Paulina, Pyotr was frustrated.

That the man had dared approach Paulina after he'd warned him against such was unthinkable.

The stakes were raised, the gauntlet thrown.

He could no longer play pacifist and wish the danger away. This was a menace that went to the very heart of him, of any man- his family. When it came to his daughter, to the sanctity and protection of his most beloved child, there were no limits to what he would do to protect her. No rules.

He must act!

His work boots and stockings were where he'd left them by the foot of the bed. His shirt was hanging loose outside of his pants, his belt unbuckled. He sat down on the bed and kicked off his slippers one by one. He poured himself more vodka.

With two hours to go, he had time to think, to stretch, to do some push-ups, to plan and look at options. He'd been tired but was now too alert to sleep. He didn't have to report for his shift until 6 am. He would leave the house by midnight. Boris Kuznetsov worked nights at a tavern on the docks somewhere. This time, he would find him first and they'd have a conversation. What happened after that would be anyone's guess. All Pyotr knew was that whatever it took, the extortion would end. The threat must be eradicated tonight.

A couple of hours later, his mind was settled and his money roll was full. He dressed carefully for the chilly night. Boots on, he reached over to pull open his night table drawer. With grim determination, he grabbed the small knife he always wore in his boot and slipped it inside its sheath. Spying his service pistol, a simple, reliable 45, he picked it up. Weighing it in his hand, he checked to make sure it was loaded and tucked it his belt. He shut the drawer as softly as he could.

Quietly making his way through the house and drawn by the light coming into her room from the streetlight outside, he could not resist looking in on Paulina. Once asleep, she was a sound sleeper. He never got tired of looking at her.

Paulina's sweet, clean scent permeated her room, as did the rosewater she used that reminded him again of Irena. He bent down to kiss his daughter's forehead, pleased she slept the peaceful sleep of the innocent, and determined that he'd do whatever he must to keep it that way.

The young couldn't know how fast life actually went by. How fleeting it all was and how foolish to take any day, any time for granted. At his age, with only older age to look forward to, feeling one's abilities diminish and watching sickness or death pick off the people you knew or cared about one by one, what was most important in life became very clear—as did, right and wrong.

◆ ◆ ◆ ◆

He found Boris Kuznetsov in the fourth tavern he stopped at, a cheap hole in the wall that reeked of greasy food and unpleasant body odors. The patrons were laborers, many of them foreign. They were a rough-looking, hard-drinking bunch, men seeking isolation or oblivion in drink or quick coin playing pool or hustling cards. There wasn't a woman, loose or otherwise in sight.

Kuznetsov, not seeming surprised to see him, was sitting perched like a bird on a rail by the door. He was isolated, alone and looking bored. Keeping his face free of expression, Pyotr issued a whispered but terse order that he would speak with him this night.

Kuznetsov grunted. He agreed to meet him in an hour. "When I am done here. At two. Where?"

Pyotr slipped him directions.

Glancing at the small paper in his palm, Kuznetsov nodded, grunting again.

Pyotr turned and left.

The night air was brisk and damp. This time of year fog permeated the near forty acres of brick barracks, warehouses, shops and all manner of ships. In the dark, the area held a faintly maleficent air.

The piss smell of river mixed with the stench of fish, decay, gasoline, and fresh paint was more pervasive in some spots than others. The naval yard was at least five miles of paved streets, interspersed with railroad spires but the smells became as unnoticeable as the background sounds of the water did; slaps against iron, the thud of wood, an occasional squawk or squeal from a disgruntled seabird, a splash or two and the pull of anchor chains with links as large as a fat lady's wrists tied taut with hemp rope as thick as a man's thigh. Sometimes one heard a horse neigh, a wagon, a human voice or two, a horn or distant whistle.

Pyotr knew the shipyards like the back of his hand. He also knew the docks, the nooks and crannies, the alleys and dead zones, the supply depots and where to go if one wanted solitude. They would meet here, amidst man-made materials that lay like ruin everywhere.

Pyotr stood in the shadows, pacing beneath the gargantuan skeletal steel of a gantry crane, the largest one of its kind. The crane, hooks dangling and long swinging arms frozen in place, hovered hundreds of feet over the carcass of a rusting battleship. The ship was awaiting service that would begin shortly but at present, was postponed because of the sub. The only light came mostly from a distant street lamp and lights that were strung high above and mounted on cranes.

The deserted ship was almost as tall as the soon-to-be demolished twenty-story Gillender building in New York. Sailors as a whole were a superstitious lot, and empty ships emanated an eerie air that kept men away. Even he had to suppress a shiver, but the meeting would be on his terms. There would be no witnesses except for any wayward spirits hovering about. The sheer bulk of the ship and her current pending status lent privacy. He'd chosen well.

◆ ◆ ◆ ◆

"Yaroslav!"

The ass! He heard the crunch of Kuznetsov's boots before he heard him call out. Sliding with ease from his resting place against the crane, Pyotr came out of the shadows, making his presence known, waiting and watching as his nemesis came closer.

The docks, three hundred to seven hundred feet long ran like veins everywhere, life lines between and by buildings and ships. Added to the mix were obstacle courses of lumber stacks, rocks, rope, mountains of steel rods and concrete blocks as large as cars and webbed with steel spikes as sharp as spears. Machines, parts or objects lay everywhere, sometimes looking haphazard but in truth an organized chaos.

Standing directly in front of Pyotr and parallel to the steel grid of the crane's side, Kuznetsov looked pleased with himself. "You vanted to see me?"

"Da." Pyotr nodded, eyes locked to Kuznetsov's whose he noted were red, glassy and malevolent.

He didn't care and pulled out his pistol. He aimed it directly at Kuznetsov's heart. "I am crack shot so would be shame if you move."

Hand steady as a rock, Pyotr spoke. "I tell you I am Marchencko, not Yaroslav, yet you persist. We never met, have no argument, I mind my business yet I ask you leave me and mine alone and you disregard. You seek to bother my daughter, to threaten me through her. I won't have it!"

Boris's chin jutted out as if indignant then he smiled like the evil villain in a penny reel. He chuckled. "Nice girl, beautiful. I did not bother."

"Cut the crap," ordered Pyotr, command rising in his voice.

He stood taller than the man by at least seven inches. Putting his face inches from Kuznetsov's wizened features, he pushed the gun into his belly and said, "I offer you last chance to end this. What is it you want? Tell me now."

With his left hand, he yanked his money clip out of his pocket and waved the wad of bills in Kuznetzov's ugly face. "Is it this?"

Kuznetzov glanced from Pyotr's face to the gun and back to the bills. He said, "What if it was? How much you willing to pay for my silen--"

"Not silence," shouted Pyotr, not in the mood for his games. "I will not tell you again, I not have secret. I just want you gone. To leave here. To go away for good. Not come back to New York or I will kill you."

"Oh yeah, some passive, religious Jew you are," mocked Kuznetsov still arrogant though seeming momentarily neutralized by the money more than the threat.

"One thousand American dollars," said Pyotr, ignoring his mockery, pushing his advantage, pushing the bills against the man's thick barrel chest as he reiterated his terms. "Remember Boris Kuznetsov, you must leave here tonight. You cannot come back or ask for more. Last chance. You take money or die. Decide!"

Kuznetsov made a face but took the bills. He yanked them out of the clip and handed Pyotr back the clip as he counted them. His eyes, yellow like a rattlesnake's, lit up. It looked as if he'd never seen so many dollars at one time. When he grunted and stuffed them in his pants' pocket, Pyotr felt some of his tension lift.

Relieved it had been easier than expected, but to be sure Kuznetsov understood he wasn't kidding,

Pyotr waved the pistol before lowering it as he said, "I do not issue empty threat. I will be worst nightmare if you ever bother me or mine again. Understood?"

"Da," said Boris Kuznetsov with a nod. "But real man no need weapon…you are coward!" Looking disgusted, he spit, turning his head to the left before turning it back to add, "As long as you understand this-"

He rushed Pyotr, closing the distance between them as with one hand, he grabbed the pistol, twisting it away from his body and then throwing it high and far like a discus while with his other hand, he punched Pyotr in the jaw. It was a powerful uppercut, and the grab like the punch was unexpected and solid.

"Another Yaroslav will not get the better of me ever again."

Totally unprepared for the impact, Pyotr lost his balance and fell, first hitting the side of his head on the metal crane, than landing flat and hard on his back.

The sound of his fall on the rough concrete was as explosive as the pain rushing through his skull was agonizing. For a moment, he thought his head had split open. He could not think or see straight. He felt as if he would throw up, but anger and adrenalin took over.

Before he could recover, Kuznetsov kicked, hitting him in the chest.

Pyotr rolled and turned, intending to push up to stand his ground, but as dishonorable a fighter as there ever was, like a ten-ton monkey on a coconut, Kuznetsov jumped on top of him.

The full impact of his solid bulk was what it must feel like to be hit by a train. The air in Pyotr's lungs whooshed out; leaving him gasping. Face down, his chin scraped the rough ground as he struggled to catch his breath.

He'd never before fought someone trying to kill him. Though he was a strong man, a skilled boxer and wrestler and knew how to hold his own in a fair fight, he hadn't practiced in years.

A dirty street fighter all the way, Kuznetsov took advantage of Pyotr being down. He straddled his back. He began pummeling him repeatedly with his beefy fists. Without pause, he hit him hard in the arms, the shoulders, the back and the back of his head.

The smell of the man, his sweat and hot, rancid

breath and the crazy look in his eyes as he rained blows on him at a rapid pace were getting the best of Pyotr. It was all he could do not to pass out or vomit. The pain in his head was excruciating. The thought of his daughter defenseless and alone if this madman succeeded in killing him was alarming. That thought alone gave him the will and the strength he needed to rally. With a roar that came from the depths, he went a little berserk too. His senses dulled to everything but survival. He swung; kicking and bucking like a captured stallion. He managed to knock Kuznetsov off of his back. Rolling to a stand, he charged him like an angry bull.

Ignoring the metallic taste of blood filling his mouth, Pyotr spit out a tooth.

Remembering his knife, he reached for it.

Just in time. Kuznetsov jumped him again, this time hanging onto Pyotr as if he were a pole. Kuznetsov had his dirty hands around his throat, squeezing him like a bartender would a lime for a vodka tonic. Fortunately, Pyotr was taller, and twirling managed to stick his attacker in the back with the knife. He thrust the blade to the hilt before pulling it back, enough to force Kuznetsov to let go of him, Before he could make him lose consciousness.

They were evenly matched in strength and determination, if not in size. Pyotr lost track of time or memory of who dominated whom as they went back and forth. It was a fight to the death now and the instinct to kill rather than be killed, kicked in.

They grappled, rolled and fought, neither going down until Kuznetsov wild-eyed, blood coming from his ear, one eye puffing and blood dripping freely from his nose and back where he'd been stabbed-- managed to crab-crawl and scramble up the crane as if it were a staircase.

The fear that a wounded and vengeful Kuznetsov might escape spurred Pyotr on despite the agony of his pounding head, the dizziness and nausea riding him. He had the advantage of familiarity, of knowing the set-up and climbing rigs and cranes. He caught up to his nemesis quickly.

With iron, concrete and the ocean swirling beneath them, they parried back and forth, ropes and booms swaying. The wind was strong at this height. Pyotr knew the steel beams were slippery in places. Kuznetsov had slipped several times already, his eyes darted nervously in various directions before he started off running on the beams as if he were a side-show tightrope walker or a thief with the police on his tail.

Despite almost losing his balance several times, Kuznetsov managed to make it to the end of one crane and jumped on another. When he did, the boom arm he landed upon suddenly swung to the right. He stumbled and, trying to right himself failed. His arms outstretched, he tried to grab onto a beam, but he missed and with a look of surprise and a shriek he fell.

Pyotr cringed at the thud of Kuznetsov's body hitting the solid ground. He didn't have to see him to know he most probably was dead, but he had to make sure. Making his way carefully to the edge of the scaffolding, he looked down and saw Kuznetsov was indeed dead. Even if the fall to the hard ground far below hadn't killed him, the spike of steel sticking up through his chest had.

Breathing heavily, all he felt was relief. All that mattered was that Paulina was safe. That was all he cared about. His daughter was safe!

He managed to make his way down the crane without incident. He retrieved his pistol behind some rocks, and with an hour and half to spare before he had to report for his shift, he sent

Kuznetsov to the bottom of the sea secured on a jagged pyre of concrete.

He was shaking and dizzy and threw up several times on the way towards his work. He was most probably concussed if the throbbing pain in his head was any indication, but he could always go to a doctor later if his headache didn't go away.

The streets were quiet, not a soul in sight. He stopped in a nearby tavern on the way to use the bathroom and clean himself off. He still felt very sick to his stomach, dizzy and weary, like if he stopped and closed his eyes, he'd never want to wake up. The urge to do just that was overpowering. His hands and knuckles were sore. The adrenalin was wearing off and he felt exhausted between the hits to his head and body and not sleeping all night. He suspected he was black and blue and bruised all over, but except for a scratch on the bottom of his chin where it had rested against the ground and a cut on his lip where he'd bitten down too hard, his face was unmarked. No one would suspect he'd been in a fight for his life or that he'd taken one. He 'd been fortunate. The threat was removed. Kuznetsov was dead.

CHAPTER SEVEN

February 1911
New York

Paulina awoke to birds singing outside her bedroom window though it was still quite dark outside. It was too early to dress for her new job as a feller hand—a seamstress at the Triangle Waist Factory. She'd taken the job and dropped out of high school before graduation because the opportunity had come and she didn't intend to be a burden on anyone, least of all her best friend and neighbor, Mina or her boyfriend, Elliott. If it weren't for them, and Elliott's family, who she was coming to like and know better than before she was alone in the world.

Both had been upset by her decision to quit school, but finishing her diploma had to wait. As her Papa always had said, people plan but life has other ideas. It wasn't as if she had aspirations like Mina who wanted to be a doctor. She didn't have a family business to inherit, like Elliott, who worked in his father's jewelry business. No, all she'd ever wanted was a simple life with her mama and papa, and to marry Elliott and have a family of her own someday. She suspected Elliott had been planning to propose after she graduated high school, but then tragedy struck and everything changed.

She glanced around her tiny, almost sparse bedroom, at her mahogany dresser with its ornate princess mirror, at the gilded, framed photos of her great aunt and great uncle, at her beautiful mother and handsome, distinguished father, all of them vital and alive. Just thinking about living in a world without either of her beloved parents made tears come, and she had no time for that. Mama had raised her to be strong, caring and practical. Papa had raised her to work to the best of her abilities, to expect the unexpected and make the best of life's surprises.

And, she would.

She blinked her eyes several times, wiping at them until any sign of her weakness left.

So many changes. Could she afford to eat, to keep

her home? What would she do? Where should she go? Forcing herself to put aside worry and grief to sort through a lifetime of family mementos and memories kept her going; deciding what to keep, what to give away. Last night she'd all but dropped to sleep out of sheer exhaustion.

She got up out of bed as agitated as the day before. Why was she nervous? Not because of the job, a job she could do with her eyes closed. Sewing was a skill her mother had taught her as soon as she could hold a needle. She was fast and accurate stitching on a machine too, so that wasn't it.

She headed towards the kitchen, a wraith in a white cotton gown padding down the hall, bare feet on hard, well-worn planked wood floors. In spite of herself, she glanced at the new elephant in the room, the pile of belongings dumped on the living room floor in denial last night. They would have to be confronted.

Papa never woke up after his injury, so she hadn't known his wishes. She preferred forgetting but could not avoid the stack of foreign looking papers.

Or the small, ornate chest she'd discovered hidden under a false bottom in her late papa's desk.

That, and a rough drawing of what had turned out

to be a diagram of the bedroom floorboards where papa, who never really trusted banks kept his money.

She hadn't been surprised to discover her inheritance there; stacks of fifty and one hundred dollar bills and silver coins, enough that if she remained frugal, she could keep the apartment and her life on course for another year or two.

It was a relief knowing she would not have to move in with Mina or feel hurried to plan a wedding in the midst of her grieving.

Paulina nervously wiped her palms and walked over to the pile of her father's belongings. She was taken aback to discover papa had secrets. Secrets. It was all so confusing.

She was scared, scared because though unexpected, this hadn't surprised her. And now, unable to deny her curiosity, she knew she must try and understand why her simple father had a hidden drawer with a locked chest that looked like something that belonged in a museum. Inside, a gray uniform with golden yellow stars and lines; a slew of official looking military service papers in Russian and a diploma from a prominent Russian University belonging to a Petya Yaroslav.

Paulina understood some Russian, but she could

only read and write in English. If she decided to investigate further, she'd have to get help with the papers, but she also had to consider papa kept his secrets for a reason.

The eerie truth was, the chest looked exactly like the one he'd described in the bedtime stories he'd told her since she was a child. She would have bet those stories were all from his imagination and that he never lied to her, but now, she wasn't so sure. Were his stories or parts of them actually real?

She strained to lift the ornate box with both hands. It was small but very heavy. And, locked. She hadn't found a key so she could not open it. Why had he hidden this? Why did he have it? What did it all mean?

Riffling through the papers, her fingers traced the strange letters as she tried to make some sense out of her find.

Papa had been well read and smart, but formally educated? She knew Petya was a pet name for Pyotr and this Petya had attended a large university for there was a graduation certificate and Russian Naval military papers with a faded photo of him. He'd been an officer and the photo showed a man, a younger version of her father? Who was this stranger, this Petya Yaroslav?

She would never be able to ask papa anything now. An accident in the shipyard. Papa had been working and just passed out. When he had, he fell far to the ground. A head injury they said. She was still troubled by it. At least they had seen her mother's end coming, but accidents were too sudden.

Looking at the dates on the papers she knew this man was no stranger. He was Papa. Papa had been him. These things, they were his—she told herself to believe it already.

The box felt warm, or was it vibrating in her hands? Was she that nervous? She bent, her intent to place it on the floor. It dropped to the carpet with a heavy thud, the sound of something inside rattled. Jewels? Gold?

Rattled, she covered it over with a sofa pillow and left it where it sat. She didn't have time to explore this mystery now. She had to go to work. She had to think about what all this meant. What to do? Who to confide in?

Heading to the kitchen, she found the honey, sliced a lemon and brewed herself hot water.

Life could be so wonderful, but it also could be

very harsh. She forced herself to focus on the now as she readied her breakfast, slicing an apple, buttering a piece of fresh bread she'd baked the day before.

The morning sun was starting to pierce through the bathroom curtain as she prepared herself for work; it shined through the small, high-set window and fell on her long, bound auburn toned hair. She resembled her mother and had her pert, tipped nose and delicate chin, but she had her father's bright green eyes, dark hair and narrow lipped smile, though her lips were much fuller than his had been.

Her mama; the beautiful Irena had been a wonderful homemaker and a talented seamstress sewing, knitting or crocheting whenever she could. And, that is exactly what Paulina felt she could do too.

She looked down to the sink as she pulled the plug and let the water out. She had to get to the bank. She had to take out the garbage. The bathroom needed a good scrubbing, but chores would have to wait. She had taken too long thinking. Only if she hurried would she be on time.

So, she rushed, stuck her sewing needles and pins into the lapel of her favorite, pink sweater. It was her mother's; one she'd knitted and sometimes when she closed her eyes, she felt as if her mother's arms were wrapped around her, comforting her. It was nonsense, but wearing the sweater always made her feel better.

Gathering her things, she put on her coat and hurried to leave and catch the trolley. She ran down the stairs, opening then closing the door to hop down the remaining twelve steps to the sidewalk, dodging the slowest of passerby's.

Who had he been then, her papa whom she'd loved so deeply? The gentle man who had called her mother Solnechniy, his sunshine, and indeed she had been.

Her mother had the kind of beauty that radiated from within, one that came from possessing the most loving and nurturing of hearts. Ironic Irena's own heart, as big and loving as it was had failed her- them, taking her away far too soon, Just ten months after Paulina had found her lying on the floor that sixth night of Hanukah, she died a year later on the first night of Hanukah.

Subsequently, Paulina refused to celebrate Hanukah because the winter holidays made her sad instead of happy. That papa had died early in January made it even worse now. She didn't even want to think about what she'd do or how she'd get through the next holiday season. She dreaded it!

She went to school and kept true to her faith after her mother died, but nothing was ever the same. She'd thankfully had papa and they'd carried on the best they could. He provided well, worked hard, went to shul on Friday nights and had been a good, loving father. Even at ten years old, while she never doubted he loved her dearly, she knew when he lost his sunshine--her mother, half of him had died too. And, now they were both gone.

CHAPTER EIGHT

I t was dark outside when Paulina returned home, sore and aching and tired. The work was more demanding than she would have thought, but she could get used to that. What she didn't like was being treated like a criminal, locked in a large room with hundreds of others, with only thirty minutes off all day long.

Her hands hurt. She rubbed them together. Her fingers were stiff and sore, her nails too short. She'd frayed her fingertips pulling seams and pins and because they were worked well past reasonable and decent hours. There was no negotiating, only following what everyone else did at those long tables, slick floors leaving residue on her shoes, and matted balls of fabric scrap piled in baskets around the room like the eyes of the dragon commandants observing and monitoring everyone's production.

She even had to ask permission to use the bathroom and if the manager thought anyone took too long, he'd threaten to cut their wages or hours. It was so embarrassing; most of the seamstresses avoided drinking.

For one dollar and fifty cents a week, Paulina worked on the eighth floor putting together the materials for the popular shirtwaists the company was famed for. The factory inhabited the top three stories of the building and employed over four hundred people.

Even with the windows open and overhead fans, the space was sweltering hot and muggy. It smelled of fabric, dyes, metal, oil, perfume and human perspiration. With spring coming, it wasn't only flowers blooming as flies breaking out of winter stasis buzzed along with the incessant hum of a hundred or more sewing machines. The noise and the rules discouraged conversation. Any violators caught talking were suspended without pay. A normal day began at seven thirty in the morning and ended at five o'clock or at peak times, nine.

Because she had so much time to think, she spent much of it wondering about the mysterious papers hidden in papa's desk and what might be in the box.

Something about the box had ingrained itself into her mind since she touched it. She also could not stop questioning if many of the stories he'd told her might have actually been true and were not just from his imagination.

When she got home that evening and the telephone rang, she was almost glad for the break. She picked up and said hello. Mina sounded tired too, but was as feisty as usual.

"How was your day at the factory today?"

Paulina sighed, trying to stretch out some of the kinks in her neck. "If I hear the word hurry, hurry, faster, faster, one more time, I will have to kick someone in a soft place with my boots on. They lock us into the room and inspect us before we are allowed to leave; afraid we might sneak off with something. It's porky, but jobs are hard to find and at least it is honest work."

"Well, I wish you would quit! You should go back to school, graduate like both your papa and mama wanted you to do. Let Elliott marry you like he is dying to do, poor boy. It is what you wanted before…what your father wanted for you too, and I want to be a bridesmaid."

She and Mina bonded at nine when Paulina's

mother passed away, and her father hired Mina's mother, Sonya to care for her before and after school when he was at work.

"Mina, one must allow the proper time to grieve to pass. I can't think about getting married until the year passes."

"That's old fashioned thinking. I understand not wanting a wedding yet, but you can still grieve and be engaged!"

"I know, but Elliott understands, I need some time. I won't do that in the shadow of papa's death."

"I understand too, but you might feel differently when more time passes. Didn't Elliott offer you a job at his father's jewelry store? Didn't he beg you to get your diploma?"

"Yes, but I wouldn't impose on the Rosenthal's like that and I prefer sewing to filing. I am fine where I am for now. I have a year to study and take the test to earn my diploma."

"Will you do it, stubborn girl?" Mina was relentless. She added. "I know how you feel, Paulie, I do. There isn't a day that goes by when I don't miss my mother too, but I also know death is part of life. We all will die. It isn't a choice of when, when our time comes, it comes. The trick is to cherish and enjoy the people and things in your life that are happy while you are living. None of us are promised tomorrow."

Mina's wisdom went beyond age and religious difference. Her logic about life and death helped.

Paulina sighed, rubbing her eyes. "You're right, but that doesn't make it easier to bear. I have promised Elliott I will get my diploma before the year is out, but I have too much to do and am too tired to do it all right now."

Sharing this type of hardship with her friend when she herself had just lost her own parent was a horrible thing. Mina's mother had died just eight months ago.

Paulina sat down on a chair and yawned. "How are you doing with school?"

"Studying constantly, worrying about tests, never enough time with my volunteer work at the hospital, the usual."

Mina stalled, and then blurted, "I didn't get the two scholarships I was hoping for. Those went to boys too since I have been told more than once, women are more interested in marriage and having a family. Am I a dodo bird wanting a University and a medical school education?"

"No, Mina and I am so sorry," said Paulina.

Mina worked hard for her grades in the parochial school she attended and had sat with a comatose Pyotr whenever Paulina needed a break. She was a natural caregiver and she'd hoped to start school as soon as possible. The medical profession was a male domicile and medical institutions encouraged men more than women.

"It's not unexpected," she sighed, sounding resigned. "People say I am chasing a rainbow."

"I don't!" Paulina was emphatic. "If anyone should be a doctor, it's you! You said there are women who persevere and become doctors. You will too."

"There is a reason why I love having you for a best friend," said Mina, chuckling. "But the truth is, the women who make it either have a father who is a doctor or money for education. I have neither. Mother only left enough for me to pay for necessities. It will be okay, though. You know me, I will keep trying even if I become the oldest female doctor in the United States."

Paulina laughed, knowing Mina meant it. "What will you do now?"

"Old Dr. Brooks has offered me a job working in

his office through summer. Maybe next year too. If I save enough money, I'll apply next year and the next after that if I have to."

They hung up and Paulina leaned into the cushioned chair. She knew whatever it took, Mina was determined to follow her dream. Thinking of dreams…the box and items loomed in her vision. What if there really was a treasure? What if she could actually help Mina somehow?

She stood, stretched. She needed answers. She couldn't even think of starting a new life if her old one was a lie! What if her father had been a spy or a thief?

Her whole being rebelled at the idea. Her father had been such an honest, compassionate, loyal and loving man. He wouldn't have done anything to hurt anyone. She sat down on the rug, uncovered the box and wondered if mama had known about the papers and the box or if papa had hidden it from her too. Now she would never know. She needed to find the key.

Perhaps the key was in the folded uniform she had dumped on the floor? Papa's desk and bedroom were the only things she hadn't explored thoroughly yet. As a child, she wasn't allowed to even touch his desk. She hoped the key was somewhere in there or in his closet.

Staring at the thing for some time, Paulina troubled herself with the next complication. There was still so much to go through. Looking at the clock on the mantel, seeing how late it was already, she knew she'd have to postpone searching for the key.

The next morning, Paulina had to force herself to get up and go to work with what little sleep she'd had.

She hurried into her cramped space and resumed what she thought she did very well. Her stitching was straight and even, she kept her space neat and worked quickly like her mother.

Another week disappeared as her work at the factory kept her too exhausted to do much more than go home, bathe, talk to Mina and Elliott on the telephone, change and stare at the messy house and all the things she still had to do but was too tired to do.

She thought she was doing well until one morning, thirty minutes early even, the floor boss yelled, "Go up a floor, we don't need ya here."

"Will I be doing the same thing?" She asked,

encouraged.

"Suppose so! Get up there. Stop wasting more time."

"May I ask why you're sending me?" Paulina pressed, curious and hopeful she was being sent upstairs because she worked fast enough to be considered one of the better seamstresses, but knew she shouldn't have spoken so freely.

He looked up with a puffed chest, "Replaced ya with someone who'll get the amount done that needs doing!"

She deflated as he turned his heavy head away from her, dismissing her all at once. "And, make sure you use the freight elevator!"

She took her things, straightened up her station and waved goodbye to her co-workers.

She wondered if she'd see Yetta and immediately found herself nervous again, but able to impress the man there; he observed her for the rest of the day, checking her stitching on the coats less and less frequently.

Returning home in the darkness, having stayed later than ever, she was glad in three days she would be spending time with Elliott. She had one Saturday off a month and they would meet for Saturday morning services, than an afternoon at the park, to see a show and supper at his parent's house. She looked forward to it. She missed seeing her friends at Saturday services and needed a break, a laugh, something to do and somewhere to be away from all the work she had left to do, all the things she had to figure out. Upon coming through her door, she did her best to ignore the mess and collapsed into bed. She sat up to rub some rose petal lotion on her blistered fingers.

She lay down again and tried closing her eyes, but felt as if someone was in the room with her. Uncomfortable, she scanned the room, but found nothing.

Until that moment, she realized she hadn't thought about the chest for several hours. The contents all came to her in a flash.

What if they were photographs from Papa's childhood! She would love to see that, and getting up, forced herself to fight the exhaustion and go look around her papa's room.

An hour or so later, she found the box as she'd left it. The latch looked sound, but iron can rust, and believing any key could fit the hole and possibly work, she used a skeleton key she found hanging behind papa's shirts in his closet. She fiddled with it for some time. To her delight, the locking mechanism crunched at the tenth turn. Bits of black and red shavings mulched out of the hole into a fine grated dust that was the lock. She opened the lid; it protested, but she protested back. In a final jolt, the hinges gave way, the lid flew open and the box fell to the floor with a clatter, some of its contents tumbling out.

What was she looking at?

She couldn't believe her eyes.

She was dreaming.

She had fallen asleep, surely!

This wasn't his—her father told her stories about treasures, sunken ships and pirate, mermaids and sirens and kings and queens, about the Czar's palace all her life.

They could not be true.

What if they were?

One story he'd told often was about a cursed treasure and a Russian battleship that sank in the Baltic Sea near Finland with almost two hundred men aboard. How one man had survived and found the treasure. Wanting to die himself, the man had swam for miles and, as his strength was waning, had come upon a beautiful sea siren who, instead of luring him upon the rocks to his death to finish him off as was a siren's wont, had reached out her hand and saved him.

As it happened, the treasure hadn't been cursed but instead blessed, and though they were from two different worlds, they fell in love and overcame all the odds and together, lived happily ever after.

The shipwreck story always made papa's eyes mist. He said it was because it had really happened and many good men lost their lives that day. Sea sirens were mythical creatures, and the one in his story always sounded identical to her mother. Tears stung her own eyes. Odd she'd just realized all this now.

She felt excited but tense.

Restless, she picked up a newspaper off the floor, dusted off the table nearest her with her hand.

She looked around the room nervously, feeling some shame that she should be questioning the stories her father had told her, remembering the stories she'd adored all her life and dissecting them; however the more she mused, the more it seemed possible the answers she sought were within her own memory if she could sort truth from fiction.

"A secret treasure filled with items stolen from the Czar's treasure room. That people had died for."

Guilt flooded her, but why should she feel guilty? It wasn't hers, but it was hers. Who else would the box and its contents belong to now?

She touched the box, stared at its contents in openmouthed disbelief. She looked away only to feel the pull to look again and again. A trembling ran through her as her shock settled. Fingers, sore from holding a needle all week, began to cramp, as did her stomach.

No!

Pyotr Marchencko had been what he seemed, a devoted husband and father. A man, who went to shul every Friday night, had close friends and worked at the Naval yard. A man of very modest means with little formal education. Yet, a man who loved to read voraciously and spoke several languages. He was quiet, a very private person; he never liked to talk much about his life before he came to America and met her mother.

Faintness tugged at her.

Going over what she knew of her father only made him sound stranger, a pirate from some other time and world . . . but what of her mother? She could not have known of this. Paulina didn't want to know either.

She grabbed the fallen treasure and stuffed it back into the box. She pushed the lid down then slammed it back on top of the box, trying to go back, to remind herself, to reassure herself she hadn't just seen so much wealth in front of her.

Mama had been a simple, devoutly religious and happy woman. They were all simple! Papa had been much older than her mother, not as devoutly religious, and as Paulina was starting to suspect, maybe never a Jew at all.

"And though they were from two different worlds, they fell in love and overcame all the odds and together, lived happily ever after."

Thinking of her father's words and the siren and the sailor story, she wondered if he'd loved her mother enough to accept her beliefs so they could live happily ever after. Oh no, she was only making it worse, finding irregularities to his character.

She thought of him and saw him in her mind's eye. He'd doted on them so. There was little he enjoyed more than relaxing each evening after supper with his vodka, his pipe, the newspaper and a good mariners tale. Nor was there a night when he didn't ask her about her day and listen to her girlish chatter or indulge her with one of his wonderfully imaginative stories.

Shaking her head, she sniffed, tears sliding down her face like a summer storm as she swiped at her face with the back of her hand then forced herself to open the box again. There were five odd looking rocks and a bunch of ancient looking coins that might have been gold, but they were dirty, some coins were dull and some shiny and there was a variety so she didn't know if any of them were rare or worth anything.

What interested her most was probably the most valuable thing in the box. It was a beautiful jeweled brooch.

She examined it in awe, turning it different ways to see how it's brilliant stones refracted the light. It was ornate and fancy, gold and diamond-encrusted, a perfect songbird with eyes so blue and shiny they had to be sapphires? Oh! She would be robbed, put in danger! Arrested!

She couldn't keep these things lying around if they were valuable, but, but . . . something tugged at her about the brooch.

Papa had told his stories and how many had

involved a beautiful diamond and sapphire pin that had once belonged to Catherine the great. The jewels in some of his stories had magical powers or a curse but she was certain he'd once talked about a brooch reputed to turn into a bird that flew between the worlds connecting the living to the dead. Was it this brooch that had somehow wound its way into papa's elaborate stories? Surely, the brooch in front of her was real and as solid as the stack of old coins it had been nesting on.

She picked it up, and in a flash saw her father staring back at her through the reflection in the shinier coins. She dropped it as if it were a hot coal.

"Papa!"

She violently turned to look behind her, suddenly frightened she would see him standing behind her, but nothing was there. And, why should she be afraid of her own papa when she'd give anything to have him back?

She attributed her nerves to exhaustion. She was so tired, not sleeping enough, not eating or drinking enough and working too hard.

She had to do something else. This place was a disgrace. She had to find the strength to empty the dirty dishwater, gather up the garbage, put away the dishes and tidy up the house. Surely, she had other things to do, surely had something to do!

She entered the kitchen, heart pounding, her vision blurry. She made herself some hot milk and put a snippet of vodka in it for good measure to calm her jangled nerves. She cleaned for as long as she could stand, sipping her toddy, glad to be doing something.

Resting against the counter edge, her eyelids grew heavy. She yawned, her body telling her it wanted sleep. She wasn't sure if she could sleep, but finally decided to go to bed while there were a few hours left. In the morning, she was meeting the loving and patient man she planned to marry.

She hid the chest in a large cabinet. Should she confide to Elliott or Mina about what she'd discovered, or wait until she knew more?

What would they think?

She had to think about what to tell or not.

She didn't want to cast aspersions on her papa's character.

She put the uniform and the papers back into the hidden drawer and closed it. Yawning and beyond tired, she went to bed.

He followed his superior officer back to his bunk, astonished when the captain ordered him to shut the cabin door behind them; the wood hammering against the steel, the sea disappearing from their ears, only the sway of the ocean still in the room.

He watched as the captain, little confidence gained with his darting nervous eyes, gently lowered the box he'd been holding, and set it down on the table with a weighty thud. His expression became fierce. Looking him directly in the eye, the captain's usually ruddy jowls quivered. His eyes were fervent and glazed as he requested he listen carefully and not speak, they only had minutes.

He said, "Ve hrrave known vun another since boyhood and I am commanding officer. You must trust vat I will tell yoo without question for there is no time left. Both of us grew up amidst seeds of revolution so we know the plots of men. Upon my Ahncle's death, it fell to me to be guardian of certain documents and items remaining from rebellion of 1825. In box are blue diamonds cut from infamous Le Tavernier, and several valuable ancient artifacts and gold coins. But the brooch! The brooch once rode upon the bosom of the Great Catherine herself! It is made from Spanish gold, Ceylon sapphires and diamonds. It is reputed to have power to connect the living...," he swallowed deeply and his voice shook, "to the dead! Those who wear it most like carry its secrets, whether treasure, or curse—I cannot say."

Reaching into his uniform jacket, he pulled out a thin goatskin packet, sealed entirely in wax. He placed it on the table by the box. "You must slip off ship ven we are away from port. No one must see. You must swim like fish. Take papers and box and see them safe until I return from voyage. If I don't return, you will have memorized name and address of person to take them to. Do this immediately if I don't return, and tell no one of this-ever."

"Of course."

Petya was uncertain why Viktor would not return or why all would not be well. He was an excellent swimmer and trained almost daily in the cold Baltic seas, but the hard part would be to sneak off the ship without anyone in the fleet spotting him. That would be nothing short of a miracle. He said as much to his captain.

"What if I am spotted?"

"Yoo won't be—can't. I know I ask of yoo a lot, but consider this a mission of the utmost importance. I have not enough time to tell yoo, so understand once. Someone tried kill me. Papers in wrong hands endanger many. Can cause another uprising. Treasure was taken from Czar's winter palace, diamond room many years ago. Some believe these objects inside were given to Paul the first, by devil himself and have much mystical powers. "

Where before he was dutifully planning how he would escape unnoticed, being a man of science, Petya could only grunt and say, "With all due respect, Captain, surely you don't believe that nonsense?"

Viktor sighed, rubbing his temples. "Ven my dreams show me my own death and those images flood my head; ven I feel salt-sea through my nose, filling my lungs and see ship going straight down on sea floor like spike, feel and hear steel buckling, see men fighting till end, all lost in ship's steel embrace, I wonder. This morning, despite storm comink, Admiral Burachecka ordered us to sea anyhow."

Petya had shivered seeing how worried the captain was. He would not risk life unnecessarily. If Viktor was the secret guardian of these objects and was feeling endangered, he understood why he would want to safeguard them. And why he'd trust him to see to it.

"It's burden. Sometimes I think better for them to disappear, but not my call to make."

Looking at his timepiece, Viktor quickly outlined his plan. He made Petya memorize the name and address of his contact should anything happen to him. He would leave his cabin door open so Petya could retrieve the items after the ship left port. He vowed to divert the attention of the crew and the following ship at just the right moment. The two men calibrated their stories and their timepieces. They embraced in a quick show of affection and luck before hurrying up deck to their stations.

Petya did as ordered. He left the ship undetected, swam to shore and remained hidden, staying out of sight as agreed until he received Viktor's call. Days later when the ship didn't return and all aboard were feared lost; he was devastated to discover Viktor's dream was a prophecy.

Weeks later, knowing he could not hide forever, he went to the address he'd been given to turn over the objects.

To his horror, he discovered the contact shot dead in his country home, a single bullet wound through his skull, his home rifled beyond measure. Stuck with the proverbial hot potato, himself presumed dead, Petya burned the dangerous papers to ash, but could not bring himself to destroy the beautiful objects. He was not a man prone to silly superstitions. Perhaps the pin brought bad luck, but he'd had the pin, not Viktor, so that made no sense. Nor had either of them been wearing it. He decided he'd keep the pin and gold coins hidden, for if they remained obscure and unworn, no one would be the wiser.

CHAPTER NINE

March 15, 1911
New York City

She tossed and turned as warmth flooded her face and heated her limbs. She kicked off her blankets, the room uncomfortably warm. Opening her eyes, only when she sat up did she feel the real chill of the room, and realized it wasn't warm at all. The dream was still with her, a vivid experience real enough to have startled her awake several times. Each time she fell back to sleep the dream continued where she left off. Her father was without doubt the Petya of the uniform and the hidden papers. She didn't know what to think but she was convinced the dream had meaning.

Maybe papa was trying to help her understand

from beyond the grave?

She got out of bed, weary but looking forward to the day ahead. She tried to push the memory of the odd dream to the back of her thoughts.

Taking time with her appearance, she pinched her cheeks a little harder. She applied more rouge than normal for she was far too pale and had lost weight.

For months she'd worn black.

She wished for the first time in weeks she could wear something with a little color, something a little more cheerful, but she was in mourning and would do what was expected and proper.

When she heard the knock at the door, the urge to share some of her burden was strong, but she knew she wouldn't tell Elliott everything—not yet-maybe never.

"Elliott!"

"Paulina!"

He looked handsome and happy. He hugged her too tight, but it felt so comforting to be in his arms after such a long time that she fell into him and molded into his lift.

As he gently set her down, arms tightly grasping her shoulders, his gaze swept over her. He looked concerned when he saw tears beading her eyes.

"Paulina, darling. What's wrong? I know these past months have been difficult and you are working too hard, but you look…beautiful as always, but frightened!" Elliott spoke softly, but his warm and beautiful brown eyes were filled with distress.

She swiped at her eyes, mad at herself for the tears. She would not do anything that could hurt her father's memory or betray his trust, she owed papa his secrets but she trusted and loved Elliott and knew he loved her. He cared for her father too. He would never do anything to hurt her. She didn't want to lie to him and it hurt her to think she might never be able to tell him all of it, but she had to share some of her concerns with someone.

She said, "I don't know what to make of it. You know I have been sorting through my parent's things. Maybe you can help me?"

She pulled him inside; she had never done that before, always behaving so circumspect and ladylike yet her aggressive action made him laugh.

"What's gotten into you, Paulie?" He asked, stepping inside further and remembering his manners, instantly pulling off his hat to hold it with both hands at his waist like a nervous boy.

She knew he'd been ready to propose after she graduated but the unexpected death of her papa changed his plans. She also knew from Mina he'd asked for her father's approval and had gotten it. Knowing one another like they did, Paulina knew Elliott understood her well enough to respect she didn't want the specter of her father's death hovering over their future. No, he didn't like that she quit school to work but he understood. He just hoped she didn't make him wait too long.

She couldn't ever consider another fellow.

She'd fallen in love with Elliott when she was only twelve years old and he, fourteen. He made her laugh and feel loved and appreciated and her papa had heartily approved of him. He had said, "a strong and promising young man, and he shows respect, and I can tell he loves you the way he should. That's all that matters to me." Papa's blessing meant everything to her.

Looking up at Elliott, holding both his hands, Paulina said, "El, I need you to promise me whatever I tell you today, you will never do anything or say anything about it to anyone without my agreement. That you will respect my wishes to do what I need to do, as I feel I need to do."

He agreed and listened in astonishment as she told him about the money she had found, about her fathers hiding spot under the floorboards and about the fancy box filled with things she believed might be valuable.

She explained. "I already took the money from inside papa's hidey hole to the bank. It is enough that if I am frugal and work, I don't have to move out of my home until I am ready. People won't think I am marrying to be supported, but for love, and I can sort through my parent's things without being rushed. I hope you understand-"

"I do, and that's good news," he said, hugging her. "I know how worried you were and knew Pyotr would have provided for you. What does Mina think?"

Looking sheepish, she said, "She thinks I should quit my job and go right back to school. I didn't tell her about this yet. I've just told you."

He smiled, hugging her again. "So, are you going to show me this treasure box you found?"

She pulled him into the living room and got the box out, but was puzzled that it was latched and tightly closed again. "I thought I broke the latch. I guess not."

While Elliott admired the workmanship on the box and remarked on its weight, she got the key. He tried to open it but this time the lock that had seemed rusty and damaged before was solid and tight and unwilling to relinquish its secrets.

"I cannot believe this," said Paulina growing exasperated as she watched him fiddle with the latch. "I swear. It opened before."

"Oh well," said Elliott, shrugging as he put the key down and turned to smooth a wayward curl from her face.

"How about we tackle this later or we will be late for services and I've a special day planned. If you'd like, we can stop by the store and I can put this in the vault. It will be safest there. I can have our locksmith work on opening it if this key won't work. Once I can see what is inside, I can better work on determining value."

She knew Joseph Rosenthal and Sons Jewelers was highly respected and a leader in the sale and design of precious stones and jewels of the highest order but felt panic blossom in her chest at the thought of giving up the box.

She shook her head no, adamant. "Thank you, I will want you to do that, of course, but not…not yet. I want to keep it here with me until I get more figured out."

His voice was patient. "Paulina, darling, if the contents are as valuable as you think, you should not keep it here for too long. If anyone else finds out about it, you're likely to get knocked off or someone can break in and take it."

Paulina waved away his concerns and patting his

cheek, told him not to worry. She scooped up the box and placed it back where she'd hidden it. "I do want your help when I am ready, but not today. Not yet. No one knows about any of this except you and I and we've never been burgled. I would like to keep the items here for now. When I decide what I want to do and feel ready to part with them, I will bring them to you."

Elliott nodded, accepting. "I appreciate your trust. I will help in any way I can, when you are ready."

Locking up the house, they headed out hand in hand to enjoy their special day together.

CHAPTER TEN

March 15, 1911
New York City

It was one o'clock in the morning and not sure what motivated her except pure stubbornness, she went out of her room to get the box. She turned on her lamp and sat on her bed trying to open it again. There was no logical reason why the key had worked once and would not work again or why it hadn't worked the first night she tried, or the third, but tonight, not being able to sleep well anyway, she decided to try until it worked. Her persistence paid off and it opened. Rifling through the contents, she couldn't quite say why, but the brooch interested her the most.

Taking it from its pillow of leather and gold, she studied it then pinned it to the collar of her nightie.

She stood to look at herself in the mirror. The brooch sparkled against the white cotton of her gown, far too fancy for her. She was a simple girl and proud of it.

Still, being a woman, she could not help but appreciate the beauty of the piece and the way the diamonds shined, emanating beams that reflected when she turned this way and that. She posed with her chin up, face haughty, using one hand to hold her hair up then letting it fall. She spun, feeling young and carefree once more and laughed at her own silliness.

Ironic she was going to marry a jeweler. She didn't dream of wearing or owning jewels and expensive baubles. All she wanted was a roof over her head, food in her mouth and the people she loved to be well and happy. Still, it was comforting wearing something her father had held special and she saw no harm in enjoying the extravagant brooch in the privacy of her own bedroom.

Yawning and tired beyond measure, she tiptoed to the bathroom. She placed the box at the far end of her bed, but kept the brooch on.

Lying back against her pillow, eyes to the ceiling, she thought about who might have worn the beautiful songbird with the sapphire eyes brooch before, who it might have belonged to. Could it be a family heirloom or was it possible, as in papa's stories, it had once belonged to Catherine the Great? Had it resided in the Czars treasure room and been stolen by disgruntled revolutionaries? Was the story of the ill-fated Rusalka a true one? Her mind spun trying to figure out what might have been said about the brooch. Did it really possess mystical powers?

She resolved that despite its beauty, she would not keep it for herself. Forget about magical powers, if she lost it, she'd never forgive herself! No, she didn't need or want such an extravagant item to sit hidden in her drawer. She would much rather have it find its right place with the right person and give Mina the money for school.

◆ ◆ ◆ ◆

It was late, and Paulina felt as if she were drifting, a growing feeling of weightlessness came and went. Heat. Cold. The air grew dense and harder to breathe. She must have a fever coming, and trying to remedy herself, gave up and let herself go, falling into a deep sleep.

Falling awake, her eyes dashed open to a black smoking void, and she couldn't move, could only watch, feel, and hear the sound of machines clacking, screams and blood-curdling cries. Smoke drifted over her vision, and a sense her father was near. She called for him.

"Papa?"

"My Paulina," he answered, love for her in every syllable.

She yearned to see him and felt his smile. "Oh, Papa, I miss you."

"I miss you too, my angel," he replied and stepped forward so she could see him, but in what a state! She felt such melancholy for his transparent form; where had he been, gone, where was he now?

"What is this?" She whispered, wondering if she were awake or dreaming, not sure.

At that, people she didn't know began to surround and crowd them. People who did not look familiar. They were dressed differently, from different times. They were getting in the way. She backed up, turned and considered pushing past them to flee but didn't want to abandon papa who stood still beside her.

First, there was a ruddy-faced, uniformed man with a beard soaked with what smelled like seawater; she recognized him as the ship captain who had given Petya/Papa the treasure and who'd drowned with his ship though he looked so placid and calm. It was like watching pictures in a nickelodeon, images flashing quickly, next a beautiful dark haired woman in such a dress, as she had never seen, the brooch hanging as a necklace around her deep cleavage, her long neck on an angled, almost haughty face of serene command. She sensed rather than saw her father. She wondered where her mother was and called out. "Mama!"

There was no answer and suddenly she was alone and scared and so warm...burning up...terrible heat!

Next she was at her new workstation on the ninth floor at the factory, the whirl of the machines deafening. She tried to work faster but it was like slogging through sludge.

Frustrated beyond measure, she felt desperate and knew she had to leave no matter the consequences.

She heard someone yell, 'Go to the light!'

She didn't see anyone, but then she saw the light.

Fire!

She ran to the door.

She tried to open it but it was locked.

Frantic to leave, she kicked it, but it would not budge.

Confused and scared, she ran, trying door after door knowing if she could not get out, the flames of red, yellow and white would claim her and everything with it.

"No. No," she screamed over and over until her voice was gone. "I am too young to die."

She lay paralyzed on the factory floor with people just piled on top of one another, all of them choking and gasping for breath as helpless to stop it, they watched the fire inch closer, taunting them all with the knowledge it would consume them.

The sewing needles in her lapel burned into her skin, glowing hot as frantic faces and blackness swirled her vision.

She opened her eyes some time later to realize with great relief it was just a dream.

She was safe in her bed. *Safe!*

She burst into tears.

Her mother! Her father! All those people.

What a terrible dream. What did it mean?

She rocked back and forth, holding herself together and feeling far more emotional than she should. It was a nightmare, not a dream and thankfully, not real!

She felt for the brooch where she'd pinned it to her gown.

Hot! Heat scorched the tips of her fingers!

Startled, she chided herself for being foolish. There were no such things as curses or magical powers. Her head was full of papa's mystery. She was being ridiculous!

Ridiculous but remembering how papa said the brooch was part of the mermaid's treasure then how the story became more obscure, changing each time he told it, until he wouldn't tell it anymore. She took off the brooch.

She kept seeing Papa in her mind's eye as Petya, then as himself telling his stories of treasure. And, the madness and evil of man, the escape of a single man with a treasure he hadn't wanted who hadn't wanted escape, and of lost comrades.

That was him! Some of the stories had to be his stories! She thought of the military garb and shuddered to think of her father almost killed on a sinking ship.

Holding the brooch in her hand, she admired its cool beauty. She told herself she must have been dreaming that it was hot, that an inanimate object could not direct dreams. Or connect the living to the dead. *Nonsense!*

Placing the pin down beside her, blankets tight around her legs, she reached for the pillow that had fallen askew and settled it back under her head. She didn't believe in such things but she'd also never had such a terrifying dream before. She would give the pin and the treasure box to Elliott for safekeeping and appraisal. As soon as possible.

Tomorrow!

CHAPTER ELEVEN

March 25, 1911
New York City

The sun was a shiny sliver rising over the blue, yellow and red horizon. The streets of New York City bustled with people going about their business and workers beginning their day. Trolleys, buggies and horse drawn carts, a milkman starting his route, a line already formed at a food cart selling delicious smelling pastries. On almost every corner, young newsboys in knickers and caps hawked papers, shouting 'hot off the press'.

Paulina got off the trolley near Washington Square Park and hurried towards the Asch Building. Glancing at a clock, she was too early and slowed her pace. After all, she didn't have to clock into work for another thirty minutes and she would still be early. She had time to breathe, to savor. She admired the beauty of having a park in the middle of the city.

Like many New Yorkers, she was numb to the crowds, and the garbage. She saw what she wanted to see; colorful stores with interesting signs, the green of the trees, the array of colors on newly blossoming buds and flowers.

Shifting the large bag she was carrying from her left shoulder to her right, she was more than anxious to shed her burden and didn't want to take it inside to work with her and chance the inspectors questioning her.

Elliott had kindly offered to meet her by the Greene Street entrance to pick it up. He'd been pleased she managed to open it again.

"Good, that saves us from involving the locksmith. We do not know why your father kept it hidden, but if it is as valuable as you suspect, I can inquire discreetly and see you get what it is worth."

"Yes, discretion is most important. Papa left me enough money to survive for some time and I am capable of work. If the treasure inside the box is actually worth something, money is always helpful to have but if I had more than I needed, my greatest wish would be to be able to help Mina become a doctor."

"What a good person you are," Elliott replied, cautioning her not to be hasty. "It is never wise to make serious decisions in the midst of crisis or grief, however if that is what you want to do for Mina, I understand, but be warned researching an item's history and worth and finding the right buyer takes time."

Paulina shrugged. "I am in no hurry. Even if I am able to gift Mina's education, she would have to apply for admission to school for next year. Still, it would make me very happy to be able to do that and surprise her."

"If it is worth something significant and I can sell it, it might be feasible you'd have it in time for Christmas."

Paulina nodded, dreading the thought of the impending holidays, but said, "Being able to help Mina would be wonderful any time."

Paulina arrived twenty minutes early at the spot where she was meeting Elliott. While the air was pleasant, the temperature sixty-eight degrees and brisk, she felt as if it were ninety degrees outside. Despite the cool air, she was beginning to perspire profusely, and concerned, decided to take off her coat.

Holding it and her bag with the box in it tightly to her side, she paced, checking constantly to see if any pickpockets were near or if she could see Elliott.

She walked from one end of the block to the other and back. She had eighteen minutes to go.

As she passed in front of the factory building the second time, her heart pounded hard and loud.

She felt as if she'd run a mile.

The sound of her own heartbeat resonated from her ears to her toes.

Taking a deep breath, she turned back to walk towards Greene Street. She started to feel even worse, as if she were spinning inside of her own body.

Sixteen minutes.

Did she have a bad heart and failing kidneys like her mother?

Having never fainted before, for a second, Paulina was sure this was it. It didn't feel painful, only interesting and jarring. She did her best to hide her fear; walking as if she had a purpose. She didn't want anyone watching to think anything was wrong with her.

A tall brick building dominated the opposite corner and seemed to grow taller as she stared at it.

She turned, pacing back and forth from her vantage point at Greene Street and Washington. Still no Elliott.

Thirteen minutes.

Passing the address marker on the front of the factory building at 23-29 Washington Place, a searing dash of heat bloomed in her pocket.

Her legs went weak, knees buckling and she staggered, reaching for the nearest wall. She pushed against it so hard she scraped her palm.

When she pulled it back, she saw she'd left a streak of blood on the cold brick.

Dizzy and nauseous, she paused feeling as if she were going to collapse from the sheer rush of adrenaline shooting through her veins. Why—what was happening to her?

With a gasp, she jumped back just in time as a woman's body hurdled from the sky, dress and fabric billowing, down, down, smacking hard on the pavement…and kept going right through the pavement.

Disappearing.

Eleven minutes.

Was she losing her mind?

Shaking, she turned to see if anyone else had seen

what she had seen but nothing was out of the ordinary then...

She screamed, stumbling backwards when another body dropped a few feet from where she had just been standing. It too disappeared.

What did she just see! What was she seeing?

Before she could answer her own questions, there were more people falling from the sky.

This could not be real!

Her hand over her mouth, she watched in mute horror as another person crashed to the ground, then another, this time a young woman she recognized from the ninth floor.

Oh no!

Dora.

Tessa.

Then a man, one she had seen in passing. He was holding onto several screaming girls who began dropping one by one. The look of horror on his face matched hers and then he jumped, following the women to his death.

She didn't think she would ever forget the screams or the terror or the dull thud sound of bodies hitting the hard concrete one by one.

Hunched against the wall as if trying to go

through it, a part of her wondered if she should warn someone, but another part was hesitant. After all, each time she looked back at the sidewalk where people had dropped, nothing was there?

The people walking by were staring at her curiously, maybe thinking she was nuts. Was she?

This wasn't real, wasn't happening.

She was either losing her mind or maybe…the brooch…she wasn't wearing it, just carrying it. Could it be giving her another nightmare even though she was awake? It had to be the brooch.

She glanced up at the building and to her shock, saw bright orange and black flames shooting out of the eighth, ninth and tenth story windows. Before she could visibly react, they disappeared.

Unable to contain her fear, she sprang from the wall and burst into a run. All she knew is she had to get away.

Nine.

She couldn't go into work today. She could be fired but she could not go!

She felt so sick, so frightened.

The thought of going back towards the factory or anywhere near that building terrified her.

She could not think!

Her gut told her not to go to work today, not to go near the factory and something was wrong with her, very wrong!

Where was Elliott? He had to be on his way.

One block down from where they were to meet, she flew across the street, running and walking and hurled herself into Elliott's arms.

Elliott's arms came up around Paulina who was sobbing inconsolably as he exclaimed. "What is the matter, what happened, did someone hurt you?"

"Oh, I am seeing terrible things," she cried shaking harder than a leaf trapped in an autumn wind gust.

She blurted out what had happened to her, what she'd seen. She knew she sounded like a crazy person, but could not calm down. "No one hurt me, but something is wrong! First I feel hot, then I see a fire and bodies falling from the sky, people I recognized, people from the shirtwaist factory. They were terrified, screaming and then jumping out of windows, it was terrible and-"

Holding her shoulders gently, Elliott stared down at her his dark eyes wide with concern and said, "Paulina, please darling, calm down, it is okay. You are safe. I can see the building from here and none of that seems to be happening."

"I know, but I kept seeing it, feeling it, a fire, all those people trapped…"

Using one hand to wipe her forehead, he exclaimed, "My God, Paulie! You are hot, burning up with a fever. No wonder you are imagining things!"

She felt exhausted, confused. "But. My work…"

"Forget it, darling. You aren't well. You have fever."

He took her bags, her coat and put his arms around her. "Come. I will get word to them. We should go to my parents' house and I will call our family doctor. He will be able to help you."

Paulina felt as if she were a train emerging from a deep dark, tunnel. She felt the rush of air around her and heard a low hum she realized were voices. She vaguely remembered what happened, the horror of another nightmare taking hold and finding Elliott, feeling safe in his arms. She knew he'd taken her to his parents' house. She heard him call the doctor but beyond that, her memories were hazy.

Someone came in the room and touched her head as gently as a butterfly's wing.

"Her fever is finally gone," she heard Mina say, recognizing her by her lavender scent before she even spoke. Then. "Are you awake, Paulina?"

She extradited herself from the lethargy pinning her down and finding her voice said, "Yes."

She blinked open her eyes to see a most welcome sight, Mina and Elliott smiling down at her and her coat, bag and the box on the chair nearby.

Elliott came rushing over and kneeling by the bed, took her hand and kissed it. His lips were as warm as his whisper. "Darling, we were so worried but thank God, you look so much better already."

"I feel much better, thank you for taking care of me, both of you. How long have I been sleeping? What time is it?

"Five o'clock," said Mina hovering close.

"What!" She sat up. She'd never slept a whole day away in her life.

Her mouth opened in shock just as Mina, never one to miss an opportunity, stuck a thermometer right into it.

Her fever disappeared with her symptoms. Even the doctor shrugged, unable to explain what it was or why it had come as quickly as it had gone.

Glad to leave the box and the pin in Elliott's care,

and not wanting to cause a scandal by remaining at his home without his parents there, Paulina insisted on returning home. Mina agreed to spend the night with her just in case of a relapse.

Once home, bathed and back in her own bed, Paulina listened as Mina told her how Elliott had called her and how alarmed he'd been. "I hope I find someone who loves me someday as much as he loves you. He is a good man."

Paulina agreed and said she felt fortunate. "I wish for you the same someday."

"Not until I become a doctor," said Mina firmly and not unexpectedly. Helping sick people was all Mina ever wanted to do since they were children.

"I know," said Paulina admitting she didn't have a strong calling like Mina did. "I not sure I have a job after today, but I don't care. I don't want to go back to that place ever again."

She told Mina she'd found her papa's nest egg and he'd left her enough money she didn't really have to go back to the factory or lose her home. "I would have told you sooner, but there never seemed time."

Mina understood and was relieved for her.

The next day, they were awakened when Elliott knocked on the door. He had been on his way to work until he'd seen the morning paper. As soon as he had, he rushed right over to tell them that yesterday at about 4:30 pm there had been a terrible fire at the Triangle Shirtwaist Factory.

Waving the paper, he looked disbelieving as he said, "One hundred and forty six people; all but twenty-three of them young women died a horrific death, but even more chilling was what Paulina saw in her delirium actually came to pass."

Mina crossed herself. Elliot looked as if he might need a stiff drink. Rushing over to Paulina, he embraced her as tight as he could. Shaking his head he looked at her and said, "Do you realize if not for your mysterious fever and delirium yesterday, you might have been inside that building when the fire occurred? You…you could have been killed too."

Paulina felt sick all over again. Elliot was right. She had no idea why she was spared when so many others, including the two young women she'd sat between on the eighth floor, Dora and Tessa were among those killed.

Mina reached for her hand, squeezing it. The three of them just stood together for minutes, paused in silence and locked in their own thoughts.

Each day that passed, people could talk of

nothing else. Paulina learned later her neighbor Yetta had been spared too. There was no logical explanation for any of it but for Paulina, already burdened with grief, it was overwhelming and she could not stop crying for days.

Mina remained close to her side and Elliott visited every day before and after work, always bringing something his mother sent for them to eat for supper.

Hugging both of them to him, Elliott said, "Special prayers are being said at synagogue for the lost. Because of this, I find myself reflecting more and more on the randomness of tragedy and death. On God."

"God does work in mysterious ways," agreed Mina as she pulled away to gather her things to go. With a perplexed expression, she admitted she had no explanation for what Paulina had experienced. Or why what she'd seen in her delirium came to fruition.

But Paulina, her father's image, his words, his hidden cache and all the dreams she had popping into her mind-- knew exactly what had happened and why. She said, "God's presence in all things noted, as crazy and unexplainable as it might sound,

I have no doubts I am here today because I was warned by papa and my loved ones and others beyond the grave and saved by one yes, very mysterious but beautiful, songbird with sapphire eyes brooch."

CHAPTER TWELVE

December 26, 1921, early evening
New York City

Shredding potatoes, slicing onions and cracking eggs, the turkey roasting in the oven since early that morning, Paulina hummed to the holiday music playing from the Victrola in the hall as she lovingly prepared the ingredients for the Hanukah latkes.

Within hours, Mina and her beau of just a few months would be joining them for supper and celebration. Both worked at City Hospital in New York. Mina was a first year resident working in the burn unit. Dr. Glenn Frank, her beau, one of the senior staff surgeons.

Paulina looked forward to lighting the candles on the first night of Hanukah with her family, and to celebrate a belated Christmas with Mina who for the past nine years was too busy studying and working over the holidays to have much time to celebrate anything.

Paulina had the table set with her finest crème laced tablecloth and Chanbord patterned china.

The gold trim and pink roses on the plates matched the crystal vase filled with imported pink roses. Roses were an extravagance this time of year and one she'd chastised her husband about, but after almost nine years of marriage, Elliott knew how to placate and spoil her. He'd said it was an early anniversary gift so she could not quite quibble.

Candles were lit throughout the house, their sweet beeswax scent mixing with the delicious smell of all the foods she'd prepared. The fresh cut, evergreen spruce and fir boughs on the fireplace mantel and the stairs brought the holidays inside. She hoped for Mina, a sense of her own childhood celebrations, too.

In addition to the roasted turkey for dinner there would be cornbread stuffing, potato latkes, mashed potatoes, cranberries and string beans she'd canned herself. As for sweets, aside from chocolates, nuts and oranges, there was homemade apple sauce, apple kreplach, honey and butter cookies with poppyseed filling, pizelle waffle cookies made with anise and tzimmes made sweet with apples, pears and plums.

Drying her hands on her apron, Paulina took a quick accessing glance at the white and blue tiled kitchen with its large counters, country sink and all the modern appliances a twenties housewife could dream of. Everything that could be ready was.

Their new home was spacious with large windows, hardwood floors and wainscoted walls of black walnut and oak.

She thought about her loved ones who were no longer here. She realized one never stopped missing those they lost, but learned to cherish their memories and life itself for it was short, mysterious and never to be taken for granted.

Paulina was convinced the brooch saved her.

She would not be alive and if not for Elliott and Mina, she would have never gotten over dreading the holidays!

She smiled, entering the living room to see Elliott finish the last of the holiday decorations by peppering the greenery with pinecones, red ribbons and popcorn strung by the children in honor of Mina's holiday, doing his best to keep the three kids out of her hair.

Whether one celebrated Christmas or Hanukah or

anything else, she'd learned every day was what you made it. The essence of every holiday was about counting ones blessings, giving and sharing and spending time with loved ones who mattered to you most.

She was shaken out of her reverie when her oldest daughter Irena shouted. "She's here, she's here."

The eight year old was at the window peering out and let go of the curtain. She began twirling spirals as if she were performing the nutcracker suite for an audience of one hundred. Her younger brother, ever restless, jumped up and down like a grasshopper on hooch.

"Auntie Mina, Auntie Mina!"

"Kids, settle down right this moment," she said trying to sound sterner than she felt. "You sound like a bunch of squealing banshees, please!"

She scooped up baby Katarina toddling at a fast pace right behind her two wilder siblings and her father just as he reached the door.

Holding the squirming child, Paulina stood by her husband and, despite the warmth of the house, felt the immediate rush of chilled air as the door opened wide.

Mina and Dr. Frank, arms bundled with gift-wrapped packages were swaddled and bundled tight as mummies. They were covered in white, a white dulled by their smiles at the sight of them and their dancing children.

"It's snowing! It's snowing!"

A new chorus of enthusiastic shouts broke out as the children saw the large snowflakes trying hard to create a picturesque winter scene on all and sundry.

Elliott helped Glenn with his bounty quickly closing the door behind them as they entered to shouts and hugs.

"It looks as beautiful in here as it smells scrumptious," said Mina with a quick hug to Paulina and Elliot as the baby practically jumped into her arms.

Mina laughed; sounding very pleased and tickling the curly haired baby cooed and said, "She's getting big and very heavy too." Taking in the touches of Christmas she knew they'd blended with their holidays for her, tears filled her pretty blue eyes as she thanked them.

Putting the baby down gently, Mina proceeded to unwrap herself; coat, hat, gloves and scarf coming off faster than cotton candy spinning at a carnival. Kneeling with arms outstretched, she braced to catch the three little rapscallions as they impatiently rushed right into their auntie's welcoming arms.

CHAPTER THIRTEEN

December 26, 1921
New York City

The evening was noisy, pleasurable, and full of food, laughter, conversation, games and gift exchanges, but like all enjoyable evenings, it flew by far too fast.

By the time Elliott pored himself and his guests another glass of wine and they had discussed everything from the state of the union, to the problems in Europe, to Prohibition, gangsters and flappers and had gone through another two bottles of wine, Mina and Paulina had cleaned up the kitchen, put the baby to sleep and had bathed the two oldest children, now playing upstairs in their rooms.

Mina had confided to Paulina that she and Glenn were heading towards matrimony. She said, "We have much in common and the same commitment to our work and very strong feelings for one another. The truth is, I have never felt like this with another human being, besides you, and this is even more than that."

"I should hope so," said Paulina laughing.

Mina looked happier than she'd ever seen her.

Her beau, Dr. Glenn Frank was in his thirties. He was intelligent, committed to his profession and had a kind and sincere manner. He insisted they call him Glenn and he and Elliott hit it off right away.

For the third time that evening, he thanked them for their hospitality.

"I am very impressed with your holiday spirit. I never observed a Hanukah celebration before and I enjoyed how you added a touch of Christmas for Mina. Longer than Mina, I cannot remember when I didn't work over the holidays. People are always sick or needing help and you probably cannot understand, but sometimes the holidays are a miserable time of year for so many so I actually like to work."

Paulina said, "I understand."

"I lost both my parents during the holiday season and if it weren't for Elliott and Mina, I would have never gotten over my dread of the holidays."

The story of the treasure box came up.

Paulina told of how it had taken Elliott almost nine months to discreetly check for provenance and figure out the value of its contents. How, as she'd guessed, all of the items were valuable.

She rubbed her hands together as she spoke. "I thought the brooch was the most valuable thing in that box, but I was wrong. Its monetary value didn't compare to the rocks, which were rare, blue diamonds or the coins, which were gold and worth the most. Some of them very old, rare and highly collectable, easily worth double and triple of everything else."

Dr. Frank was fascinated. When she explained in more detail, he said, "Surely, you wanted to keep such valuable heirlooms in your family rather than sell them?"

"No, not at all," said Paulina with a shake of her hand. "I nor my papa had any sentimental attachment to the items inside the treasure box. You might even say it was a burden. I wanted Elliott to keep the stones to make his beautiful jewelry since he would not take payment for all his hard work on my behalf. He agreed to keep only two if I'd keep the brooch."

At that, she exchanged a loving and knowing gaze with her husband before continuing.

"Being a jeweler's wife, Elliott hoped I might feel differently about keeping the brooch so he purchased it for me himself, but I didn't want to wear it. He kept it in the store vault."

Looking lost in memories, she helped herself to a cookie. Took a bite, chewed and swallowed. "More than anything else, I wanted money to help Mina with her schooling. That to me was more satisfying than owning a fancy trinket I never felt right about wearing."

Elliott reached to his wife and affectionately rubbed her arm. "And more than anything else, I wanted Paulina to get her diploma so I could honor my promise to her father and marry her."

"Well, obviously I did," she teased as smiling, she told him with all the pressure from Mina and Elliott and knowing how much it had meant to her parents, she'd completed the work for her diploma. She then invited her husband to tell the story of what had happened next.

Nodding, he sat forward and looking more than a little proud, explained how he'd suggested to Paulina she throw Mina a little holiday surprise party as an excuse to gift her with the money.

He said, "It was already early December. I knew if Paulina had something to plan, she might not have time to dwell on her grief or think about the coming holidays. Mina and I were both concerned. Mina suggested the only way to make the holidays happy for Paulina again would be to overlay her sad memories with very good, happier ones."

Elliott and Paulina exchanged several loving glances as he told how he kept Paulina busy planning Mina's surprise, and how the surprise party Paulina thought she was planning for Mina turned out to be a surprise party for herself too.

"Again, with Mina's encouragement, I got down on bent knee and proposed to Paulina in front of all our family and friends."

Dr. Frank and Mina exchanged affectionate gazes as he chuckled in amusement and said, "Why am I not surprised, Mina is involved. She excels at helping people whether it is in the hospital or out."

They all agreed and laughing, Paulina held out her hand to show Glenn the ring Elliott had designed for her using one of the rare, blue diamonds.

"Beautiful ring," said Glenn, admiring the small

square cut blue diamond surrounded with delicate rows of tiny regular diamonds. "I am impressed with your craftsmanship, Elliott and the story."

He asked if anyone minded if he lit a pipe, and no one did.

Elliott lit a cigar and Paulina brought them both an ashtray.

Setting up his pipe, Glenn looked a bit puzzled and said, "Mina has told me all you've done for her and I admire the close relationship you all share. As a doctor, I am a man of science but one of my personal interests is studying things that often cannot be explained by science. In other words, I am fascinated by how you believe the brooch may have saved you by keeping you from work on the day of that terrible factory fire at the Triangle Shirtwaist factory."

Paulina, having confided in both her husband and her friend her feelings about that day, explained.

"I was deep in my grief and busy sorting through a lifetime of family memories and stories I'd been told as a child. I wasn't taking care of myself properly and was having trouble sleeping and strange dreams. I wanted to give Elliott the treasure box for safekeeping and evaluation. That morning, the day of the fire, we were to meet before my shift at the factory. I got there early."

Mina confirmed they'd never figured out a reason for Paulina's sudden illness or a suitable explanation for why Paulina had foreseen what would happen that day.

Paulina admitted she hadn't had any unusual dreams or visits from the dead since. She said, "I know it sounds unusual and far-fetched, but I do believe the brooch does have special abilities. Any time I wore it, I felt strange. My papa used to tell me stories about a bird that had the ability to connect the living to the dead. I have reason to believe many of his stories contained truth."

Glenn acknowledged her statement and said, "I truly believe some people are more sensitive to experiences like that as well."

Elliott admitted that as a jeweler, he'd studied gemstones and throughout history people believed certain ones held special healing or magical properties. Showing support for his wife, he held her hand and said, "While I admit there may be something to it all and I believe what Paulina experienced was real, I am not inclined to accept that the cause of her experiences were all brought about by a brooch. However, I do agree there is no plausible explanation for what occurred the day of the fire and since many of Paulina's papa's stories have turned out to have some base in truth, who am I to say different. Life is full of mysteries that cannot be explained."

"True," agreed Glenn. "And I am ever glad for that. It makes life interesting and even science and sensible, logical men will admit the unexplainable does happen. Do you perhaps, still have this mystical brooch? I would love to see it.

Elliott shifted in his chair and shook his head. "No, Actually I do not. My wife convinced me to part with it and I did, just about two weeks ago. Paulina never warmed to the idea of wearing or keeping it and a few years ago, I began displaying it in a special case in the store with a not-for-sale sign on it."

"It just so happened; we got a customer about a month or so ago who decided he had to have it. The fella was a tough character, a gangster I'd guess by the looks of him. Not someone you'd want to make mad at you. He wanted it for his girlfriend. He wouldn't take no for an answer! Said she had eyes the exact same color as the songbird and was in fact, herself a singer, a songbird. He insisted it was meant to be. Said he had to have it for her.

"I told him it was an old family heirloom of my wife's and not for sale, but he insisted everything was for sale at the right price. He was quite convincing and a bit intimidating, but I was moved by his devotion to his gal so I said I would talk to my wife about it. He wouldn't budge until I called Paulina."

"I told him to sell it," said Paulina her green eyes twinkling. "Might as well have someone enjoy it, but I only wanted him to sell it with the condition he tell the buyer my experience and the whole story that came with it."

"Did you?" asked Mina and Frank in unison.

"Yes," said Elliott, rolling his eyes.

He relayed how he told the man that even though he had no papers to prove it, Catherine the Great herself reputedly wore the brooch. That it had mystical powers that could connect the living to the dead. That it could make its wearer dream. "I told him what happened to Paulina and what she thought."

Glenn asked. "What happened? What did he do?"

Elliott snorted. "First, he looked at me like I was

nuts. He said, 'So you're sayin' this pin has a curse?'

"I said, not a dangerous one necessarily, but yes, possibly.

"He laughed. He said he didn't believe in crap like that. Said he wasn't superstitious. I agreed to sell it to him, but there would be no refunds if he changed his mind. He told me not to worry. He pulled a roll of bills out of his pocket like I'd never seen one man carry. He counted out ten grand in one hundred dollars bills and it was a done deal."

Paulina, as immersed in the story as all of them were, jumped up when she heard a noise from upstairs. She glanced at the time. "It's the kids. Time to get them tucked into bed. Please excuse me."

Mina said she'd finish cleaning up and began to clear the table.

"That really isn't necessary," insisted Elliott. "Paulina won't want you doing that. She won't even let me employ a live-in or a live-out housekeeper to help her."

"Of course not." said Mina, laughing, as she chased the two men off. "I know Paulina enjoys tending to her loved ones herself and no amount of money will ever change her course or her, as you well know."

"That I do," Elliott agreed, not at all displeased as he led Glenn towards his den to show him his gemstone and rock collection.

Mina finished cleaning up the table and the kitchen and when she was done, she tiptoed up the stairs.

She didn't want to excite the children or wake them if Paulina had already managed to get them to sleep.

Seeing a dim light coming from Irena's room, she paused and smiled as she heard the two older children begging for a bedtime story.

"Mama, please, just one story, just one, please."

Paulina sounded tired but resigned. "Just one and a very short one at that."

A soft girlish voice. "Mama, the one about the princess and the magic bird."

A much louder voice. "No! I want the one about pirates and treasure."

Paulina's voice was patient but firm as she admonished her son and said, "Petya, we must speak softly as to not wake the baby. Tonight, I am going to tell you a story about real treasures, those of family and friends and the truest meaning of the holidays."

Moving closer, Mina smiled to herself as she heard the rustle of the children settling in, listened to the creak of the oversized rocker and savored the cadence of her best friends lovely voice as rolling with each rocking, she began.

"All over the world, there are all kinds of beliefs, celebrations and holidays, but the most important thing to remember is, one must never stop believing...in magic, in mystery, in the love of family and friends, in the good of people and in the hope and wonder that is our Universe and God..."

AUTHORS NOTE

As a writer, I am a stickler for weaving true history into each of my stories so when the idea came up to write a holiday anthology with a tie in to my other books, I was inspired, but not really sure how to begin.

Mermaid's Treasure is based on two true historical events; a Russian battleship that sunk off the coast of Finland and the New York Triangle Shirtwaist Factory fire. Because my 'thing' is to always weave in real history, people, places and situations these two events became the anchors. Because of my own Russian ancestry, the meaning of the name, Rusalka and the fact its sinking inspired a statue of an angel to be erected that still stands today and that I have found within my own family genealogy, gaps, contradiction and secrets not handed down, the beginnings of a story started to emerge.

Add to that my love of holidays and I was off to a good start!

I truly believe whether a holiday is based on religion, spiritual values, a person or a sentiment, it teaches traditions and ideals worth looking at. At their simplest, holidays give us the liberty to rejoice, to share and appreciate family, friends and those things we do love. And, they can make an ordinary day special!

One only has to listen to squabbling between family members (usually at get-togethers over the holidays) as they discuss childhood and recall memories differently to know like any thought or idea whispered down the lane, stories change.

If your ancestors were immigrants, they were leaving behind one life to create another. They had reasons and secrets that most likely, died with them. So, the only stories that do survive are those others tell of them or what they actually chose to share that got passed down and even that is suspect.

Speaking of passing down, I also enjoy perusing antique shops. The objects left behind or discarded by those long gone fascinate me. I often wonder if those objects could talk, what stories they would tell.

<u>Some other interesting historical facts:</u>

-In 1893, the journey the Russalka took that fateful day was an all day crossing from one Russian naval port to another, whereas today it is a two-hour express ferry service between the capitals of two Baltic countries.

The granite Angel statue erected in 1902 on Kadriorg Beach in Tallinn to honor the lost sailors of the Russalka still stands today.

-(Reference Chapter Seven) The gray in color, large hooked beak dodo bird with feathers attached to its tail was a flightless relative of the pigeon family. Because it had no natural enemies it quickly was driven to extinction around 1681 when man and animals came to the island where it originated. The name dodo bird became an expression synonymous with rarity and extinction.

-(Chapter Seven) The 'Le Tavernier' diamond was talked about as far back as 1668 and is in part the stone in modern times referred to as the Hope Diamond. It had a colorful history of royal and wealthy owners, including Louis XVI and Marie Antoinette. The original stone was a rare blue diamond that glowed red when exposed to ultra violet light. The diamond was reputed to have been cut down in size from the original larger stone over the years and acquired a reputation for bringing its wearers ill luck, though there is no real proof that was so. Today it resides on display at the Smithsonian Natural History Museum in Washington, DC.

The Triangle Shirtwaist Factory Fire was the deadliest workplace accident in New York City's history. A dropped match on the eighth floor of the clothing factory "sweatshop" famous for the popular shirtwaist styles worn at the time, sparked a fire that killed over a hundred innocent, mostly young immigrant women who were trapped inside. This brought well-deserved attention to labor violations that would forever affect the private industry and practices of American factories.

<u>Thank you for purchasing this Book.</u>

A shorter version of this story is included in the Windtree Press Anthology, The Gift of Christmas. In both versions of 'Mermaid's Treasure' you will learn more about the origin of the very special, perhaps magical diamond and sapphire brooch featured in my debut novel, 'The Songbird With Sapphire Eyes'. This brooch again reappears in the highly anticipated sequel, "Anthony's Angel."

Please contact me and/or stay tuned for release dates, etc. at www.annabrentwood.com

Reviews matter and are appreciated. Please consider leaving one.

ABOUT THE AUTHOR

Anna Brentwood grew up in Philadelphia amidst a large family of colorful characters-think Godfather, Yentil or Meet The Fockers. She especially enjoyed meeting and marrying her hero, a former Navy Seal because not only did he save her from her mother's diabolical attempts at matchmaking, he gave her two beautiful children, a menagerie of animals and fulfilled many of her greatest dreams.

Contact Anna at www.annabrentwood.com or

CONNECT via social media.

Like her on Facebook at:
https://www.facebook.com/pages/Anna-Brentwood/447346295303805?ref=hl

Twitter.com @annabrentwood
Pinterest.com/annabrentwood
Google.com/+AnnaBrentwood

www.ingramcontent.com/pod-product-compliance
Lightning Source LLC
Chambersburg PA
CBHW050452110726
47899CB00003B/913